'So the cool, detached Nurse Friday is interested in my personal life...'

Jessica jerked her head up. *'No!'* It was a vehement no.

Oliver's black arched eyebrows went up. His hands tightened around hers, pressing them harder against the warm mug.

'No?' His voice was husky. 'Why not, Jess? I'm interested in yours.'

NURSE FRIDAY

BY
MARGARET O'NEILL

MILLS & BOON®

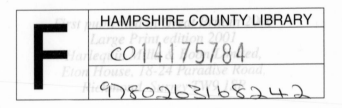
© Margaret O'Neill 2000

ISBN 0 263 16824 7

Set in Times Roman 16½ on 17½ pt.
17-0201-53825

Printed and bound in Great Britain
by Antony Rowe Ltd, Chippenham, Wiltshire

CHAPTER ONE

THE advertisement read:

Required for a Private and NHS practice: mature, experienced Registered General Nurse (other qualifications advantageous). This is a solo post. Applicants must have special caring qualities enabling them to work in this mixed environment. Ability to fill this post reflected in generous salary. Handwritten replies, CV and references to Dr Oliver Pendragon, Berkley House, Berkley Gardens, Porthampton, Hants.

Jessica was intrigued. She fitted the requirements, was a mature thirty-four, had more than one qualification and was very experienced. But a solo post! Did the generous salary mean that one nurse was expected to do the work of two? Was Dr Pendragon, in fact, a mean employer?

Well, the only way she was going to find out was if she applied for the job. She gazed out across her parents' garden and over the rolling hills of the Devon countryside. With the acute trauma of the last eighteen months behind her, it was time she flew the nest again, away from the supportive sympathy of parents and friends.

Right, she would tell Mum and Dad that she meant to apply for the post. They would be sad to see her go if she got the job, but would understand her need to re-establish her independence. And working in Hampshire, with only Dorset between, would be a plus. She would be able to visit home at any time, which would take the edge off her departure.

From the window of his elegant Edwardian house, Oliver Pendragon watched his last interviewee, Jessica Friday, arrive in a modern little black Mini and park on the gravel drive.

'Neat,' he murmured, approving her economy of movement as she halted square on to the semi-circle of manicured lawn, opposite the porticoed door. 'Unfussy—like it.'

He wasn't scornful of women drivers, but some of the women he'd interviewed earlier had made a meal of parking—a nonsense, considering that the spacious drive only contained his Rover and Rachel's Fiat. Some had been over cautious, some carelessly coming to a halt at unlikely angles, whilst the over-confident Miss King, driving a souped-up sports model, had parked in a spurt of gravel—the tyre marks were still there and had exited leaving the door swinging wide.

By and large, Oliver had found, wryly amused by his discovery, that their parking skills had been reflected in their various attitudes when he'd interviewed them. Charitably, he had presumed that some of them had been nervous or, like Miss King, falsely over-confident, but the sad fact was that none of them had matched up to the paragon he was seeking.

Or was he expecting too much of any woman to cover two practices? One a rich practice, the other a poor one. Sophie had managed but, then, Sophie was special—she would be a hard act to follow. Would Ms Friday fill the bill, match up to Sophie? He'd liked her letter of application, liked her clear, bold handwriting—but there was that matter of a gap in employment. He hoped she would be able to clear that up.

The driver's door of the Mini opened and a pair of long, slender, silk-stockinged legs swung out.

Oliver hissed his appreciation and watched as first hands appeared, holding a pair of heeled court shoes, and then a downward-bent, silver-gold head. The earlobe-length hair gleamed in the late afternoon September sunshine. Flat driving shoes were exchanged for the heeled court shoes. The flatties were thrust back into the interior and the hands reappeared, holding a black shoulder-bag.

A tall, slender figure slid out of the box on wheels, and Oliver had his first full view of Jessica Friday.

She was reed slim, and this was emphasised by the tailored black suit, in dramatic contrast to the smooth bob of hair. He couldn't see her features plainly from this angle, but had the impression of calm, classic beauty.

She stood by the car for a minute or two, her eyes roving over the gracious façade of Berkley House. As her gaze travelled along the ground floor and then up to the floors above Oliver drew back out of sight behind the velvet curtain framing the window of his consulting room.

Did she approve or disapprove? he wondered as she continued her cool inspection. His consulting room was to the far left of the front door, giving him an oblique view of the sweep of gravel. He thought she was frowning. She hesitated for a further moment and then briskly crossed the drive to the front door.

Oliver discovered that he had been holding his breath, and let out a huge sigh of relief— for a moment he'd thought she was going to get back into her car and drive away.

Before ringing the bell, Jessica paused to read the shiny brass plate on the pillar beside the door: DR OLIVER PENDRAGON MD BS DOBSRCOG—FRCGP.

She raised her eyebrows. So, as well as the expected doctor of medicine and bachelor of surgery, he had a diploma in obstetrics and gynaecology, and for good measure was a fellow of the Royal College of General Practitioners.

Not bad, a fellowship and a speciality. Neither came that easily. And a consultant GP and a one man practice apparently. Dr Pendragon must have worked his socks off and be cracking on a bit to have achieved all that.

He wasn't 'cracking on a bit,' she discovered a few minutes later when she was ushered

into his consulting room by his stunning receptionist.

Rachel Royal was as tall as her own five
eight—taller, with her coronet of red hair. Her
plum-in-the-mouth voice and willowy ele-
gance matched the lush surroundings.

The excessively well-modulated voice irritated, and at the sound of it Jessica's heart,
which had plummeted when she'd turned into
Berkley Gardens and had first caught sight of
Berkley House, sank further. She hadn't
known quite what she'd expected, but it wasn't
this opulence.

Berkley gardens, a semi-circle of houses
ranged round a crescent of railinged shrubs
and lawn, opened onto the seaside promenade.
Brass plates flanked Regency front doors,
all seemingly occupied by medical special-
ists. They shrieked of money and privilege.
This was top-of-the-market medicine,
Porthampton's answer to Harley Street.

True, the advertisement had mentioned NHS
as well as private patients, but she couldn't see
NHS patients fitting into this set-up.

'The voice' was introducing her. 'Miss
Jessica Friday, Dr Pendragon.'

The doctor uncoiled himself from the padded chair behind the magnificent antique desk and stood up, all six feet plus of him. He murmured a thank you to Rachel, who gave both him and Jessica a toothpaste-gleaming smile, before sliding gracefully out of the room and closing the door softly behind her.

His hand outstretched, Dr Pendragon leaned across the desk to greet Jessica. His back was to the light from the wide, high window behind him and she was unable see his face in detail, but she could see that it was long and lean, like the rest of him.

'Good afternoon, Miss Friday.'

Like the voice, thought Jessica as her hand was clasped in a firm grip—deep, cultured. Well, of course, it would be, she reminded herself dryly. It matches the conservative suit, the rich silk tie, the sumptuous surroundings.

'Good afternoon.' She returned the slight pressure of his fingers with a momentary tightening of her own.

The doctor released his grip and waved to the comfortable padded chair opposite his. 'Please, do sit down.'

'Thank you.'

He sat down as she did and picked up a sheaf of papers that Jessica recognised as her letter, CV and references.

'I've been reading these with great interest,' he said, glancing down at them and then across the desk at Jessica. His eyes were grey, piercingly bright and intelligent. 'You're very well qualified, midwifery as well as your general registration. Though I see that most of your nursing has been done in a hospital in the East End of London as a senior sister in A and E, not in midwifery.' There was a query in his voice.

'Yes, I wanted midwifery experience, but didn't want to specialise in it.'

'Preferring the rough and tumble of Casualty!'

'Yes.'

'But you wouldn't object to a little midwifery if it came your way?'

Jessica was startled and it registered in her voice. 'Why, is it likely to? You didn't mention it in your advertisement.'

The doctor's expression didn't change, but his grey eyes seemed suddenly chillier. 'I did say that a second qualification would be an advantage. Midwifery could be useful. I cover maternity cases in both my private and NHS practices, some of them home deliveries. I work with a regular team but, you never know, the unexpected could happen. I might want help with the occasional case. Would it bother you if I did?'

Jessica felt her stomach tighten—would it bother her? Of course it wouldn't. She was a nurse, for heaven's sake. Surely she was capable of squashing her personal feelings to do her job.

She shook her head, and Oliver was entranced by the way her hair glinted in the late sunshine splashing through the window.

'Of course not,' she said firmly.

'Good, such a pity to have a qualification and not use it.' He glanced back down at her CV and she noticed a few grey strands in his jet black hair. He raised his head. 'I see that for the last few weeks you've been working as a team nurse in a West Country health centre, but prior to that, you hadn't worked for over a year.'

He met her eyes and raised an eyebrow which spoke volumes. 'Any reason that I should know of to account for the gap, Miss Friday?'

She had known it would come and had prepared her answer, the truth, but only half the truth. Jessica made herself meet his eyes without flinching.

'I was involved in an accident in which I was injured and somebody...' She cleared her throat. 'Somebody died.'

'Somebody close to you?' surmised the doctor, his voice deeper, kinder.

So kind and gentle that just for a moment... She nodded, but found that she couldn't speak. She felt tears pricking and tried to blink them back. Damn, this wasn't meant to happen. She'd rehearsed the speech often enough.

'Here.' Dr Pendragon thrust a large handkerchief across the desk. 'Have a good blow,' he said softly. 'It helps.'

Jessica accepted it with a murmur of thanks and blew her nose hard. It did help!

'Thank you. I'll launder it and send it back.' She tucked the handkerchief away in her shoulder-bag.

The doctor's mouth quivered at the corners. 'Don't bother—the loss of one hanky won't leave me handkerchiefless.'

I bet it won't, thought Jessica, not with your sort of lifestyle. An image of a drawer full of beautifully ironed white squares next to a drawer full of immaculately ironed shirts floated into her mind. Ironed by a devoted wife? What a ridiculous thought to have in the middle of a serious interview. She ignored it.

'Nevertheless, I shall return it duly washed and ironed.' Lord, she sounded prim.

The piercing grey eyes were brilliant with suppressed amusement. As if he's read my thoughts? Jessica squashed a blush that was rising in her cheeks.

He inclined his head and said gravely, 'Thank you.' He sat back in his chair and rested his chin on clasped fingers. 'Now…do you feel like carrying on?' His voice was still kind.

I must have blown it, she thought. He's just humouring me. No way would he want to employ a woman who dissolves into tears at the drop of a hat. Oh, well, might as well go through with the charade if he's willing.

'I'm quite ready, thank you,' she said, producing a smile. 'You were asking me about the gap in employment…'

'And you explained that it was on account of having had a serious accident. Fair enough, it's not in the least surprising that you needed time off to recover. There's something else I must ask because you will need to drive in connection with your work—were you responsible for the accident, Miss Friday?'

Jessica's brown eyes met his grey ones head on. 'No, I was not. It was caused by a drunken driver, and I have a perfectly clean, valid driving licence.' Her voice was firm, positive.

The doctor held her gaze. She had beautiful eyes, like rich brown velvet with a hint of amber. Warm, honest eyes, eyes to reassure nervous patients. 'Right. Now a few more questions… Why didn't you return to hospital work when you were fit enough? Why the short spell as a practice nurse in Devon?'

'I felt I needed a change of direction after all that had happened, a break with my old hospital. To be honest, I was undecided whether to continue with nursing at all. The practice nursing was just a fill-in whilst I was sorting things out.'

She smiled a quirky smile, and Oliver was surprised to see a small dimple appear beside her mouth. Her eyes glinted amber. 'As to

Devon, my home is there, and my father's head of the practice where I'm working. And I find that I like practice nursing, which is why I answered your advertisement.'

The grey eyes searched her face. 'And I wouldn't be stealing you away from your work and your home if I offered you the job here?'

Jessica raised a quizzical eyebrow and said dryly, 'No, of course not. But that's not very likely, is it, considering what a fool I've made of myself, getting emotional? As for my parents, they know that my stay at home is only temporary. They've been wonderfully supportive since the accident, but I want—need—to be independent again. Regarding the job, it was only to cover summer holidays and the bulk of those are over.'

The dimple appeared again and her voice was warm with affection. 'Though I dare say Dad would have found me the odd job to do had I needed it.'

Oliver returned her smile. 'A little nepotism is not necessarily bad,' he said dryly. 'Depending on the circumstances.'

He found himself wanting to know how and why she'd lost her independence in the first place. What would have made a self-contained,

well-qualified career woman of thirty-four
throw that away to return home to live with
her parents for over a year? For a short spell,
yes—but a year?

What sort of trauma had she suffered in the
accident? There were no obvious signs of
physical injury. Of course there might be hidden scarring, internal injuries, or else it was
deep emotional trauma. Had she felt guilty because she had survived and somebody else had
not? That was a common scenario in accident
cases.

Deep in thought, he kept his head bent over
her CV so that she wouldn't see the questions
in his eyes. There was no doubt that apart from
this gap in her working life—and she'd explained that almost to his satisfaction—her CV
and references were excellent. In fact, everything about her seemed satisfactory. The held-
back tears were a blip and she'd soon recovered. He'd have bet his bottom dollar that she
didn't readily give way to tears.

She was as near a match to Sophie as anyone could be. Her svelte slenderness and so-
phistication would suit his private patients, and
the kind eyes indicated that she would be car-

ing with his patients at the other end of the social scale.

No one else had come close to fitting the dual role. The private side of his practice and the salary had interested most of the other applicants. He couldn't imagine any of them dealing patiently with the elderly, fumbling arthritics and grizzly children in his Arundel Street practice, whereas Jessica Friday was used to dealing with the rough, tough customers in an East End casualty department. His Arundel Street practice would hold no terrors for her. And gut feeling told him that she would be kind without patronising them.

Jessica watched the bent head in silence. He was obviously disturbed by her outburst and not really satisfied with her answers about the gap in her life. She was on the point of calling an end to the farce when he looked up and again met her eyes across the width of the desk.

'Would you like to see my NHS surgery?' he asked abruptly.

She was nearly thrown by his abruptness and the invitation. A wave of hope surged through her—he wasn't dismissing her out of hand.

She said breathily, 'I'd love to. I wondered where you saw your NHS patients—it's obviously not here in these sumptuous rooms.'

Oliver felt a stab of disappointment. Was there a note of reproach in her voice, reverse snobbery? He hadn't thought of that possibility. He said sharply, 'Why, would it be a problem, nursing my private patients?'

Jessica was surprised and indignant. 'Certainly not, Dr Pendragon. Whatever gives you that idea? Everyone's entitled to medical care. I'm a nurse, I care for anyone who is sick—*anyone*. A patient is a patient. A sick rich child suffers the same as a sick poor one, and they both need plenty of TLC. That's an important factor which seems to be in short supply these days.'

Again she gave him that direct look from her velvet brown eyes. 'And, don't forget, I've grown up in an overworked GP's household. My father's practice is a very mixed one—county types, farm workers, OAPs, down-and-outs—there are no distinctions. It's not all rural bliss down in Devon.'

She sounded angry, and her pale cheeks had flushed to a pleasant shade of pink. She went on. 'It's just that so far what I've seen here caters for one end of the market only, and I was beginning to think that maybe the NHS side of your practice was a sort of Cinderella, of less account than your private one.'

Oliver heaved a mental sigh of relief. She'd passed that test with flying colours. She was so obviously angry and astonished by the suggestion that she might be prejudiced. Perhaps she *was* another Sophie.

He looked at his watch. 'Nearly five. The waiting room will be filling up for evening surgery…'

Jessica looked disappointed. 'Oh, in that case, I suppose you'll have to rush off. I thought perhaps you meant that we could visit now.'

'I do. I've got an assistant in Arundel Street—he's on duty tonight. Nice young chap, Rory Black, finished his hospital stint a few months ago. Wanted GP practice experience before doing a spell with the VSO in the spring. He's very reliable, learning fast.' He stood up. 'Let's go. I'm afraid it'll be a lightning tour as I have an appointment later, but you'll have a chance to see the surgery in action.'

Rachel was on the phone when they passed through the elegant reception hall. She waved a languid, beautifully manicured hand as they reached the door to the vestibule leading to the front door.

The doctor paused by her desk and said softly, 'Push off as soon as you can. I'll be at Arundel Street for the next half-hour, showing Miss Friday round.'

Somehow, between talking and listening, Rachel managed another dazzling smile, and her blue eyes lit up. She gave Jessica the thumbs-up sign. 'Looks like you're in,' she mouthed.

The friendly gesture from the sophisticated receptionist surprised Jessica, and the words stunned her. Was she 'in'? she wondered. Suddenly, in spite of her uncertainty at the start of the interview, she wanted to be in, to be part of this dual practice, working beside Dr Oliver Pendragon.

The doctor grinned at her as he held open the front door and stood aside for her to pass through. His eyes, she noticed, crinkled at the corners. 'Rachel surprise you?' he asked.

Jessica nodded. 'She looks so perfect and the smile's quite something. The thumbs-up doesn't match first impressions.'

Oliver's grin turned into a chuckle. 'Current boyfriend's a dental surgeon, which accounts for the teeth. I think she has no end of free scaling and polishing. But she's a great girl beneath the elegant poise. I think you'll get on well together.'

Another broad hint that he was going to offer her the job? Should she ask? No, perhaps not. She'd wait till she'd seen the other surgery. She clamped her lips tightly together but couldn't stop her heart giving an excited jolt. It would be good to be back working full time again.

They were now outside and Jessica made to cross the drive to her car. 'We'll go in mine,' said the doctor, taking her elbow and steering her across to the dark blue Rover. His hand felt pleasantly strong, warm and firm beneath her arm. She rather liked the sensation. 'It's not far, but there's a lot of traffic about this time of day and a maze of streets as we get near the docks—you might lose me.'

The drive across town took about twenty minutes. The doctor was a good driver, moving away from traffic lights smoothly, weaving round other vehicles when possible but not taking any risks.

Jessica sat back in the leather comfort of the seat and relaxed after a few minutes, something that, since the accident, she had found difficult to do in a strange car. Yet she felt safe with those sinewy, competent hands on the wheel. She slid a glance up at his profile. What a strong face it was, the aquiline nose quite prominent above the thin line of his mouth and firm jaw.

He turned his head slightly and gave her a brief, sideways glance. A smile touched his lips and warmed the grey eyes for an instant. 'All right now?' he asked, as if he had sensed her earlier tenseness.

'Fine,' she replied.

'Good.'

They drove the rest of the way to Arundel Street in silence.

CHAPTER TWO

ARUNDEL STREET was a long street of tired-looking terraced houses, survivors of the turn of the century. A few were spruced up with window boxes, most looked as if they could do with a paint job. Any exposed piece of brickwork was daubed with graffiti. Towering over the street on all sides were high-rise flats, grey, faceless buildings. The difference between this and Berkley Gardens, only twenty minutes or so away, was breath-taking.

'That's the surgery,' said Dr Pendragon, cruising past a pair of houses which had obviously been knocked into one. There was a brass plate, surprisingly shiny, beside the double entrance door, claiming simply in large letters that it was a doctor's surgery.

No name, no list of qualifications, noted Jessica. She wondered why they hadn't stopped outside the surgery.

'We have a large ethnic community,' explained the doctor, reading her mind. 'Names and fancy letters mean nothing to many of them. Some come with interpreters, often second-generation kids or those who are learning English at school.' His mouth curled up at one corner. 'Makes diagnosis interesting, to say the least.'

He turned into a side street and then turned again into a cobbled alleyway behind the terrace. He stopped outside a pair of padlocked, high double gates and fished a bunch of keys from his pocket.

'When I'm doing visits,' he said, 'I use an ancient banger like Rory's that was parked out in front. A battered old vehicle stands less chance of being vandalised than something like this.' He patted the Rover's polished dashboard. 'When I'm in this, I park in the yard—it's reasonably safe there. You'll have to do the same with your Mini,' he added as he got out and crossed to the gates.

Jessica felt her chest tighten, and she breathed in and out very fast. Another casual remark suggesting that the job was hers. This time she had to ask.

'Are you saying,' she said, as he returned to the car and slid into the driving seat, 'that I've got the job?' Her usual husky voice came out rather high.

The doctor drove into the yard, stopped the engine and turned to face her. 'You know,' he said, a smile touching his stern mouth, 'I rather think I am.'

'Well…' Jessica let out a pent-up breath. 'I think you might have asked if I wanted it, rather than assumed…'

One of his hands covered her clenched fists. 'But you do, don't you?' he said, his eyes fixed steadily on hers.

A mixture of emotions swirled round her mind. He should have asked her formally, they hadn't even discussed salary and duties involved, he was taking too much for granted… But he was right—she *did* want the job, end of story.

She gave in gracefully. 'Yes, I rather think I do,' she said simply.

The whirlwind tour of the surgery didn't take long.

The waiting room was already half-full. The plastic and iron frame chairs were shabby, having been repaired in some cases, and were placed in uniform rows. It made sense, trying to cram a lot of chairs into a small space. There was no room for niceties, such as low tables

with magazines, though there were a few battered toys piled in a basket near the door.
There were black and dusky faces as well as
white, and men in turbans, women in saris.

There was an air of resignation about the
patiently waiting people, ranging from babes
in arms to weathered-looking elderlies.

They were, in fact, the same sort of mixture
that filled the reception area in East Central,
thought Jessica. There was the usual hum of
conversation in several languages, hacking
coughs, grizzling babes and, over all, the usual
sweaty smell of a lot of bodies sitting cheek
by jowl. She felt immediately at home. This
was familiar territory.

The doctor called a general good evening
and waved a friendly hand as he led her to the
reception counter. A few hands were raised in
return and several smiling or curious faces
turned toward them.

'You're being given the once-over,' murmured the doctor.

The receptionists—two middle-aged
ladies—behind the counter were dealing with
patients. The doctor waited till the queue
cleared to introduce them to Jessica.

'Miss Friday, meet Mrs Jane Gee and Mrs Dorothy Carter,' he said. 'Ladies, you'll be seeing quite a bit of Jessica—she's about to join us as practice nurse.'

This is the first time he's called me Jessica, she thought as she shook hands.

Dorothy gave her a beaming smile. 'Welcome to the nut house,' she said.

Jane ran her eyes over Jessica's immaculate black suit and said with a sceptical little half-smile, 'As Dot says, welcome to our neck of the woods—rather different to Berkley Gardens, isn't it? To say the least, we're not as genteel.' Her eyes said Jessica didn't have a hope in hell of staying the course in this tough neighbourhood.

Before Jessica could utter a word, Dr Pendragon replied for her. He, too, had read the message in Jane's eyes. 'As a matter of interest, Jessica's been working in the casualty department of a hospital in London's East End for several years.' He leaned over the counter and spoke directly to Jane. 'And it doesn't come much tougher than that.'

Jane reddened a bit, but grinned. 'Oh, well, in that case, you're very welcome, Jessica. We won't have to wet-nurse you.'

Jessica laughed. 'That's for sure,' she said, 'but I'll be glad of a guiding hand while I find my feet.'

The rest of the visit passed in a flash—not that there was much to see: the reasonably equipped treatment room with a barred window, where Jessica would work; a shabby but homely staffroom with a sink, a kettle and mugs on a Formica worktop running beneath the window. Both faced out onto the yard, as did the staff loos. The general office—a mere cubby-hole—and two doctors' offices were on the opposite side of the passage.

She met Rory Black in one of them. He was as Dr Pendragon had described, too young-looking to be a fully fledged doctor. He had a kind, chubby face beneath a thatch of wild, sandy hair and was obviously full of energy and enthusiasm. Pumping Jessica's hand up and down, he wished her a really warm welcome, adding, 'You'll love it here, it's great. Interesting mix of patients and a nice bunch to work with.' He gave the older doctor a sly grin. 'And the boss isn't bad either.'

Poker-faced, Dr Pendragon growled, 'Don't you ever forget, lad, that I hold your professional future in my hands.'

A few minutes later, after glancing at his watch, the doctor whisked Jessica along the passage past a flight of dark stairs to the back door leading to the yard.

He nodded toward the stairs as they passed. 'They lead up to the flat occupied by Fred Stone—he's the caretaker and does odd jobs both here and at the Berkley surgery. Handy sort of chap to have around, can turn his hand to anything.'

A thin, short, wiry man, who could have been anywhere between thirty and fifty, was vigorously polishing the Rover.

He grinned as they crossed the yard. 'Hi, Doc.' He nodded to Jessica. 'Miss… Thought I'd give the old girl a bit of a go-over.' He stood back and looked at the gleaming vehicle critically. 'But she needs a proper do. I'll see to her tomorrow at the house.'

'This is Fred,' said the doctor. 'The Rover is his pride and joy. He expends more TLC on it than we're able to give the patients. Fred, this is Miss Friday, our new nurse. You will be meeting up with her both here and at Berkley House.'

At the end of Arundel Street, they joined the inner lane of traffic streaming up from the docks. The sun was low in the west, and the golden sunshine was hazy with exhaust fumes. There were huge container vehicles as well as buses and cars, all emitting their contribution.

'This,' remarked Oliver Pendragon, waving a hand at the battered lorry with a smoking exhaust in front of them, 'doesn't help our asthmatics or bronchitics, and we've plenty of those. The Asians seem to be particularly prone. And this is a low-lying area with sea mist creeping in from the harbour. It can be lethal in the winter.'

'Do you have many deaths from chest conditions?'

They were at a standstill, and the doctor turned to look at her. His face had a raw, sad look about it. 'We do,' he said. 'Too many, particularly amongst the very old and the very young. They still come from places like India or Pakistan without any idea of the difference in climate, still hoping for jobs, a better life. Many of them don't find work and live on a subsistence allowance, as do, in fact, some of the home grown population, who are no better off. This is the poorest district in the town.'

He heaved a heavy sigh and smoothly pulled off again as the traffic began to move forward.

'It can be pretty grim and in a practice like ours we meet up with it daily. We try, but one so often feels helpless. Ulcers, broken bones—everything takes that much longer to heal where there's poverty in the house. And in the winter there are deaths through hypothermia. Yet amazingly most of them manage to keep fairly cheerful.'

'But at least they get some sort of health care and you do what you can for them,' said Jessica, 'though I can see what an uphill struggle it is. You must notice a vast difference between the patients in your two practices. Do you sometimes wish—?'

The Rover jerked to a halt, throwing her against her tightening seat belt and then whipping her back again, leaving her breathless. She was aware that the doctor had shot his hand out protectively across her waist.

Simultaneously there came the sound of clashing metal and breaking glass from somewhere ahead of them, but they couldn't see anything. The lorry in front of them blocked their view.

A shudder of fear shook Jessica from head to foot. An accident—she was involved in another accident... She clamped her teeth and lips together tightly. She *wouldn't* scream.

'Sorry about that.' The doctor's already deep voice was a tone deeper. He was breathing heavily, his hand remaining protectively on her stomach. 'Are you all right Jessica?'

She closed her eyes for a moment and took a couple of deep breaths, then opened them and nodded. 'Yes, thank you.' To her surprise, she found that her hands were pressing his hand that lay across her stomach, holding it there, comforted by its warm pressure. She snatched her hands away and felt colour stealing into her pale cheeks. 'I'm fine now,' she said her voice firm.

He lifted his hand. 'Good. Now, I'm going to take a look at what's happened. I doubt that there's anything too bad, we were moving too slowly. You stay put.' He reached behind his seat and pulled out a medical bag and square leather box marked 'Oxygen'. 'Lifeline— never go far without this,' he said with a tight smile.

Jessica released her seat belt. 'I'm going with you. After all, I'm a nurse, I might be useful.' She was pleased that her voice came out firm and resolute.

Later she was to recall that he didn't try to dissuade her—she was grateful to him for that.

He gave her a very direct look, his grey eyes assessing her. 'OK, let's go.'

There were people getting out of their cars in the middle and outer lanes. Some were talking into their mobiles, some calling to each other. A couple of men, the bumpers of their cars locked together, were shouting abuse at each other.

'Let's hope,' the doctor murmured as he and Jessica pushed their way between the groups of people, 'that the accident is no worse than that.'

Their hopes were dashed when they reached a cluster of cars some five vehicles in front of them, slewed at angles across the road, blocking all lanes. There was glass on the road from broken head- and taillights. Several drivers were standing by their cars in stunned silence, looking at the damage in obvious disbelief.

The driver of an articulated lorry, which had been in collision with one corner of an ancient Morris Traveller, was climbing down from his cab. He reached the ground and leaned against it, looking pale and shaky.

'We'll start with the Morris—looks as if there might be a problem there. Nobody else looks to be in serious trouble,' said the doctor, edging his way towards it.

There was just room between the front of the lorry, where it was jammed into the back and side of the car, to push round it. It was at right angles across the road, almost touching the car in the middle lane, but there was room for them to squeeze through. The doctor placed his case and the oxygen down on the ground and eased open the door of the Morris.

There was an elderly couple in the car. A man was slumped over, his head turned sideways, resting on the steering-wheel, straining against his seat belt, and a woman was in the passenger seat. The woman appeared unhurt. Her eyes wide and frightened, she was staring straight ahead. The doctor crouched down beside the driver.

'You look at the woman,' he instructed Jessica. 'Check for whiplash—they've had a severe jolt from the back.'

The engine was still running and he turned off the ignition as Jessica sidled round the front of the car between it and the side of the car in the middle lane. Dr Pendragon was taking the driver's temporal pulse as she opened the door on the passenger side. There was a blue line around the man's lips and he was breathing noisily.

The doctor looked up and into Jessica's eyes, and pulled a face. 'Not good,' he mouthed. 'Heart attack, I guess.' He undid the seat belt, eased the old man carefully back from the steering-wheel against the seat, and reset the seat into a reclining position.

Jessica suppressed a ripple of fear and made herself concentrate on the woman. Please, don't let him die, she prayed inwardly. She put a hand on the woman's shoulder and bent to speak into her ear. 'Do you hurt anywhere, love?' she asked gently.

The woman didn't answer, but continued to stare straight in front of her as Jessica took her wrist and placed her fingers over the radial pulse. The beat was fast but strong, with no indication of an internal bleed which would have weakened it. Quickly she ran her hands down the woman's legs. Nothing, no visible signs of injury or broken bones.

With extra-gentle hands, Jessica ran her fingers round the rigid neck. Except for the rigidity, it felt normal, with no bones out of place. She glanced across at the doctor. 'Have you got a collar in your case?' she asked.

The doctor was frowning as he examined the driver's chest with his stethoscope, listening intently. 'Yes.' He was terse. 'Come round and fetch it and open up the oxygen, please.' He glanced up quickly. 'How's your lady—anything else beside a possible whiplash?' He bent his head again to examine the driver's eyes.

'Shocked, but otherwise I think she's all right.'

'Good. Touch and go with this old boy, I'm afraid, though the oxygen might help.'

Jessica threaded her way back round the car to the driver's side. She was opening the oxygen when the woman moaned and mumbled, 'Arthur, where's Arthur?'

Afraid that the woman might move suddenly and further damage her neck, Jessica thrust the small oxygen cylinder at the doctor, collected the collar from the case and squeezed her way back to the other side of the vehicle. The injured driver had to be Arthur.

'Arthur's here. You've had an accident, and a doctor's with him,' she said, bending down and leaning into the car so that she was facing the woman. 'Please, don't move, you've hurt your neck. I want to put this collar on to support it and stop you doing any more damage.' Swiftly she slipped the collar round the rigid neck.

The woman stared at her uncomprehendingly. 'An accident!' Sudden panic filled her eyes. 'Is Arthur all right?' she whispered. Her hand clutched Jessica's arm.

The doctor interjected quickly. 'I'm Dr Pendragon. We're doing what we can for Arthur, Mrs...?'

Realising that she couldn't turn her head, the woman turned her whole trunk round so that she could look at him. 'Watts,' she breathed. 'Ruth Watts.'

Her eyes flickered down to the reclining figure of the driver. They filled with tears. 'Today's our golden wedding anniversary. We've been visiting the dockyard... He's an old navy man, you see.' She touched her husband's cheek beside the mask. 'Is that oxygen you're giving him to help his breathing?'

'Yes. You've seen him having it before?'

Ruth tried to nod, found she couldn't, and whispered, 'Yes.'

'Tell me, Mrs Watts, has Arthur got a bad heart?' The doctor's voice was soft and gentle.

'He's got angina, but it's not bothered him for ages.'

'Does he carry tablets with him in case of an attack?'

'Sometimes. If he's got them they'll be in one of his top pockets.'

Arthur's eyes flickered open as the doctor began searching through the pockets of his jacket. With a little moan, he lifted his hands up to the mask, struggling to pull it away from his face.

'Leave it where it is, old chap,' said the doctor, taking hold of the scrabbling hands. 'It's oxygen, helping you breathe. You've had a bit of an accident and a bad attack of angina. I'm looking for your glyceryl trinitrate tablets.'

At the sound of the calm, firm voice, a puzzled look, followed by awareness and then fear registered in Arthur's eyes.

His chest heaving painfully, he struggled to sit up. 'Wife—where's my wife?'

'I'm here, love, right beside you. I'm fine.' Ruth touched his cheek again.

With a grunt of relief, Arthur collapsed back into his seat.

The doctor found the tablets in a slim container clearly marked. As he was popping one of the tiny tablets under Arthur's tongue they heard the sound of an ambulance approaching.

By the time they had given the paramedics details about the two patients, and the road had been cleared enough for the traffic to get moving, it was after eight o'clock. It was dark, except for the amber streetlighting and the headlights of the streaming columns of vehicles.

They drove in silence for a few minutes, mulling over their thoughts and the events of the last hour or so. Then the doctor spoke abruptly.

'Thanks for your help back there. Must have been rough for you after your own experience not so long ago.'

'At least there was no blood. Last time...' She shuddered violently.

His hands tightened fractionally on the wheel. 'Do you want to talk about it?'

Did she? Would it be a relief to talk to this near stranger, this man who had proved that he could be warm and gentle in spite of the piercing eyes, the cultured voice, the tailored suit, yet who, unlike her loving family, was distanced from her?

She'd never been able to tell her family or close friends everything. Her palms began to sweat. She rubbed them down her smooth black skirt, and down over her knees. There were holes in her stockings. Of course, she'd knelt down beside the car when talking to Mrs Watts.

'I wonder how they are?' she said, through clenched teeth.

If the doctor was surprised that she'd ignored his question, that her voice had a hard edge to it, he didn't show it or pretend that he didn't know who she was talking about.

'The old lady will be OK once she's over the shock, but Arthur? His heart was all over the place. I'm pretty sure he's had an infarct, and it's going to take a while to straighten him out—that's if he makes it.'

Jessica felt tears sting her eyes. They were partly for the old couple, and she acknowledged honestly, partly for herself and her own precious loss.

'How sad, and on their golden wedding anniversary, too.' The tears were in her voice.

A warm hand covered hers for a moment. 'But to be together for fifty years and still have a loving relationship, that's some achievement. Whatever happens now, Mrs Watts will have wonderful memories to look back on—that's got to be a plus. Whereas there's almost something obscene when a child or a young person dies...' His voice trailed off for a moment, then hardened. 'To say the least, the sheer waste of it shakes one's faith.'

His hand was back over her white fists. He pressed them gently and rubbed his thumb over her cold knuckles. 'I don't know about you, Jessica, but although my faith gets shaken pretty often it never quite breaks. We're lucky, of course, in our profession, for although we often see the worst that life can throw at us we just as often see the best—wouldn't you agree?'

They were driving along a wide, tree-lined road leading eastwards toward the affluent outer suburbs of the city and Berkley Gardens.

Through a blur of tears Jessica stared down at the lean, strong hand covering hers. Were doctors and nurses lucky? Did seeing the best of human nature compensate for seeing the worst? Did it make up for personal heartbreak, for the appalling emptiness left by the death of a loved one, the ever-constant memory of a small scented body, the endless tears that wouldn't stop flowing?

Had working for the last few months helped her, given her any solace, any satisfaction, or had it simply filled in the long, meaningless days? Is that why she had applied for this nursing job? She honestly didn't know. Her natural compassion hadn't entirely deserted her, but how much did she *care* deep down what happened to the patients? Would she apply her skills, zombie-like?

She had known nurses who worked like that, treating nursing as they would have any other job, taking one qualification after the other to reach the top. She despised them. That sort of nursing was not for her. She believed that nurses and doctors *had* to be involved with their patients, practise detachment when they had to, but never be afraid to show that they cared.

Of course, they shouldn't be afraid. Of course, she cared as much as she ever had—only it was a caring overlaid with greater understanding, more depth. She had more, not less, to offer her patients. And the doctor was dead right. The bravery, the sheer goodness and determination of some people, patients and relatives and friends, was awe-inspiring. Nothing could outweigh the losses, but the goodness balanced the books to some extent.

They had completed the journey while her thoughts had raced, and were turning into the drive before she answered.

Swallowing the anguish, she said croakily. 'Yes, you're right. There must be as much goodness as evil in the world, and we are in the privileged position of meeting up with it from time to time.'

The headlights of the Rover, as they swept round the lawn, lit up a sleek, silver grey Ferrari already illuminated by the orange glow of the porch light.

'Oh…my…God,' breathed the doctor, 'Lucinda!'

His voice registering appalled surprise, the expression on his face broke the tension of high emotion that the accident had triggered. To her utter amazement, in spite of the painful heart-breaking remembrances of the last few minutes, Jessica found herself almost smiling. Of course—his date.

It was strange that this cool, sophisticated man should be so shattered because he was late for a date, and late for a good reason at that. He must love this Lucinda person a lot, though under the pressure of the accident he had apparently forgotten all about her. Well, that was medicine. It was a job that took one hundred per cent concentration. Surely his girlfriend, fiancée, whoever, knew that.

'Your date, I presume,' she said dryly.

He heaved a huge sigh. 'Yep, afraid so. Look, I was going to ask you in for a coffee but…'

'It's all right, I don't mind,' said Jessica. 'I'm anxious to get back to my hotel and bath and change.' And eat, she thought, recalling that she'd skipped lunch in anticipation of the interview.

Then she had been full of trepidation. Not about how she should present herself at the interview, but about her reasons for applying for the job. How much did she want it? Would it help her come to terms with her self-loathing and bitterness? Had she still got what it took to be a good nurse?

Now she had answers to all three questions. She wanted this unusual job with this man as her boss in this dual practice, though God knew how he managed them both, and helping others might give her back some self-respect. And there was no way she could be anything but a good nurse—nursing was in her blood.

The doctor's voice broke into her thoughts. 'So, please, be here by nine o'clock tomorrow morning, and we'll talk contracts and I'll introduce you to the rest of the team. Is that all right with you, Miss Friday?'

Jessica felt a stab of disappointment. They were back to Miss Friday again, the warmth and closeness of the past couple of hours behind them. Because Lucinda was nearby? He'd switched on the interior light and turned to face her. His eyes, a few inches away, stared into hers. His voice might be brisk, formal, but his eyes were a soft, bluish grey.

Jessica broke eye contact and fumbled with the release catch on her seat belt. 'Nine o'clock tomorrow morning, that'll be fine.'

'Here, let me.' The doctor pushed her clumsy fingers away and snapped the catch open. His arm brushed against the soft curve of her breasts as he withdrew his hand.

'Thanks.' Jessica opened the door, climbed out of the car and made for her Mini, fishing in her shoulder-bag for her keys as she walked.

To her surprise, the doctor was striding across the gravel beside her.

Half amused, half irritated, she said sharply, 'I don't need an escort to walk a few yards.'

They reached the car. She bent and jabbed ineffectually at the lock, silently grinding her teeth at her clumsiness. This was not *her*.

He took the keys from her. 'I thought you might need help to unlock the door,' he said, a smile in his voice as he turned the key smoothly.

Jessica bit back a smart retort and slid into the driving seat. She held out her hand. He dropped the keys into them.

'Drive carefully,' he said softly. 'See you at nine in the morning.'

'I'm looking forward to it,' she said. She started the engine, put the car in gear, drove round the semi-circle of lawn and out through the wide gateway.

Oliver Pendragon stared thoughtfully after the Mini. 'And so am I, Miss Friday,' he breathed. 'So am I.' Turning on his heel, he walked slowly toward his front door.

CHAPTER THREE

'RIGHT, Mrs Lowell-Smith, Nurse will help you get dressed and then we'll have a chat.'

Oliver removed the earpieces of his stethoscope and patted the plump arm of the overweight but elegant elderly woman lying on the couch. With a brisk nod to Jessica, he let himself out of the examination room and returned to his consulting room next door.

Mrs Lowell-Smith smiled and nodded, but turned a suddenly anxious face to Jessica as he firmly closed the door behind him.

'Do you think Dr Pendragon's pleased with me?' the old lady asked in her light, girlish, breathy voice. 'I *do* hope he thinks I'm fit enough for my operation. I can't go on much longer with this hip—it really is agony, you know.' Her faded eyes filled with tears.

Poor old thing, thought Jessica as she gently eased the plump arms into the sleeves of the wildly expensive pure silk blouse. She's as rich as Croesus, but pain's pain however rich you are. It wasn't a world-shattering revelation, but it had been surprising how often it had been illustrated in the weeks since she had joined the practice. And stoicism, or lack of it, seemed to be equally shared by rich and not so rich alike.

'Yes, I know how painful it is,' she said softly, as she lowered the couch. 'I've nursed a lot of people with arthritic hips. They are the very devil, but at least there's a cure—unlike some conditions. My grandmother, who's ninety-four, has had both of hers replaced, and she's positively bombing along now.'

The elderly face cleared a little. 'Yes, everyone says that the effects are marvellous. If only the doctor would give the go-ahead. Do *you* think that I'm fit enough, Nurse?'

'Well...' Jessica was cautious. It was always a tricky question, this, playing a sort of balancing act, not knowing for sure what the doctor's assessment would be. Not wanting to dash hopes, yet laying the ground for possible disappointment.

He hadn't said as much, but she had a suspicion that was the role that Oliver meant her to play, that of confidante, go-between. That's why he always closed the door between the two rooms when he'd finished examining a patient.

She smiled at the old lady, a warm, reassuring smile. 'You have lost another couple of pounds, though you haven't quite reached your target. But your blood pressure's stabilising nicely. Dr Pendragron's going to take that into account. But if he does want you to wait a little longer, it's because he believes that to be the best and safest course for you. Believe me, he won't make you wait a minute longer than necessary.'

And doesn't have to, she thought wryly. When he does decide, he'll be able to whip this nice old lady off to a private clinic with a wave of his magic wand. Well, she was glad for her, but— She cut off the memory of a similar case in Arundel Street, another old lady who'd waited months and would be waiting months more for a replacement.

Mrs Lowell-Smith gave a little sigh as Jessica helped her off the couch. 'Yes, of course. I have every faith in his judgement, Nurse. He's a wonderful doctor and handsome as well, in spite of that slight bump on the bridge of his nose. In fact, I think that makes him look more approachable, dependably craggy, don't you, Nurse?' She gave Jessica an arch woman to woman glance.

That was exactly as Jessica saw him, but it wasn't part of her brief to discuss his looks, craggy or otherwise, with a patient.

She resorted to being rather prim. 'He's a splendid doctor,' she endorsed briskly. That *was* part of her brief, to promote his medical skills. She handed the elegant old lady her ebony walking stick and offered her arm. 'Now, let's go and beard the lion and find out what the verdict is,' she added with a smile, gently squeezing the soft arm that was tucked into hers.

'I've decided,' said Oliver a few minutes later, 'that we can think about an operation in a week or so's time. Your heart, lungs and blood pressure are all behaving reasonably well, but you must try to lose another pound or so before then.'

Mrs Lowell-Smith's plump face lit up. 'Oh, I will, Dr Pendragon, I promise you, even if I have to starve. The thought of having this beastly thing done is the only incentive I need.'

Oliver grinned. 'Don't overdo it or you'll be too weak. Just carry on with the exercises and diet as before. I'll get in touch with Sir Richard Grenfell—he's the orthopaedic surgeon who'll be operating on you at the Nightingale—and he'll arrange an appointment to see you within the next few days. Now, is there anything else you wish to know?'

The old lady shook her beautifully coiffed head. 'You explained everything to me before. I just want to say thank you for looking after me so well and seeing me through the last few months.' She inclined her head toward Jessica. 'And thank you, too, Nurse, you've been very kind.'

It's easy to be kind to a nice grateful old thing like Mrs Lowell-Smith, reflected Jessica, tidying the examination room whilst the doctor escorted his patient through to Reception. Not so easy with some patients, rich or poor. Aggressiveness wasn't confined to the East End of London, or to unemployed youths with rampant hormones. In its own less obvious way, it was alive and kicking just as much in Berkley Gardens as in Arundel Street.

She checked the list Oliver had left for her after she'd gone off duty last night. He was sometimes already doing home visits, or making a round at the general hospital or clinic,

when she arrived for work in the mornings.
The man, in fact, was a workaholic. Again she
wondered why he was managing both a private
and NHS practice. Either one would have been
enough for most doctors. He'd started the
Arundel Street practice about five years ago,
according to Rachel, out of the blue.

It was amazing that he found time for a social life but, again, according to Rachel, he did,
and much of it with Lucinda Grant. Obviously
it was the Lucinda with whom he'd had a date
on the night of her interview, but whom she
had yet to meet.

'Are they what you might call an item?' she
had asked Rachel, idly curious about the
woman who had rattled the apparently un-
shakeable doctor.

'*She* certainly thinks they are, and she's no
dumb blonde, though she looks the part. She's
Dresden-doll tiny, with china blue eyes and
long blonde hair, the sort men, especially big
men, go for. But she's a high-flying computer
expert who knows exactly what she's about,
and at the moment her sights are fixed firmly
on our Oliver,' Rachel had replied, wrinkling
her perfect nose. 'I'm not sure how the boss
feels about her. He's what you might call en-

igmatic—doesn't give much away about his private life.'

'Yes, I had noticed,' Jessica had confirmed dryly.

That conversation had taken place a few days after she'd taken up her post and she'd still had to meet the elusive Lucinda. She had learned that Lucinda was the daughter of Lady Grant, an impressively rich patient and an indefatigable fundraiser for local good causes. Was that why Oliver Pendragon was interested in Lucinda, because her mother was a supporter of the teaching hospital where he worked?

With an angry snort she brought herself back to the present and consulted her list again. Whatever the man's interest in Lucinda Grant, it had nothing to do with her.

The next patient was a Mr Roger Jefferson. Dr Pendragon had made a note beside his name. 'New patient. Full examination, including rectal.' She was getting used to his terse notes giving her the information she required to prepare for his patients.

A rectal, though, was unusual for a new patient, unless there was anything suspect. Had Mr Jefferson a haemorrhoid problem, polyps, or something more sinister? Jessica wondered as she laid up the gleaming steel trolley with relevant items for a general and specific examination—fine rubber gloves, lubricant, bowls and wipes for the rectal. A urine-collecting carton which the patient would use in the adjoining cloakroom. Sphygmo and stethoscope for blood pressure, auroscope and ophthalmoscope for ears and eyes, patella hammer for reflexes, and a thermometer.

Another pair of disposable gloves, swabs, vials and a syringe for blood tests she placed on a separate tray. Sometimes the doctor took blood himself, sometimes he asked her to do them on the spot or in her clinic room across the corridor.

When Oliver made a full examination, he did just that—nothing was left to chance. It was easy, of course, where money and time was no object. Not that he short-changed his Arundel Street patients, though resources there were finite. He took time and trouble with them. Jessica was realising after just a few weeks that he was, in fact, a remarkable doctor.

He was also an aloof man, distant, though never with his patients. But, as Mrs Lowell-

Smith had said of the little bump on his prominent nose, these small imperfections made him more human. It was part and parcel of the man who ran the disparate practices of Berkley Gardens and Arundel Street.

It was as if he had two characters. That of the well-heeled, polished private consultant who whipped his patients into the luxurious Nightingale at the drop of a hat, and the embattled GP struggling to get hip replacements and heart surgery performed against the might of officialdom. Wearing either hat, he was revealed as a caring medic, but he was certainly a hard man to understand.

She stood back and double-checked that everything needed was present and correct, then covered the trolley with a clean white cloth. Satisfied that all was in order, she left the suite by a rear door and crossed the thickly carpeted corridor to the clinic room. This was *her* special domain, where she would wait until buzzed for. Sometimes the doctor wanted her with him when he examined a patient, sometimes not. It depended on his and the patient's needs.

*   *   *

While Jessica was busy in the examination room, Oliver Pendragon was standing at the window of his consulting room, staring out across the golden gravel of the drive. It was a favourite position when he had a moment free, enabling him to see the comings and goings of patients and staff. It was a place where he could think, mull over decisions he had made and occasionally, as now, delve into more personal matters.

At this moment he was thinking about Jessica, half professional, half personal thoughts. He could hear her moving about next door. He could picture her, cool and slender in her sophisticated lilac uniform, with a scrap of starched lace perched on her bob of silver-gold hair. She would be moving with her usual quiet assurance as she laid up the trolley in preparation for Mr Jefferson's examination.

Oliver breathed in a deep satisfied breath. It had only been a few weeks but, as far as he could see, Jessica Friday was going to be every bit as good as Sophie.

So far, he'd never seen her irritable or short with patients, however difficult they were, and they had their share of difficult patients in both practices. Some, his mother would have designated as trying the patience of a saint—but patience appeared to be Jessica's strong suit. Not that it was always a yielding patience. It was underpinned by a quiet toughness.

And she was not only good with the patients. The feedback he was getting suggested that she was striking the right note with her colleagues at both surgeries.

Rachel liked her, and had declared that they hit it off just fine. 'Jessica's great,' she'd said. 'Fun. I like her very much.'

And a few days ago he'd come across Fred in the Arundel Street yard, polishing the little black Mini. It was hard to believe that Fred was capable of blushing, but he had when Oliver had appeared. 'Hope you don't mind, Doc,' he'd stumbled out, 'but I finished the Rover and had a bit of polish left on the cloth.'

Oliver had curled up his lip. 'And it would have been a pity to waste it,' he'd suggested.

'Yeah, that's about it,' Fred had agreed.

Oliver smiled now at the memory. Fred was obviously a willing slave. As was Rory, he suspected, his eager boyish face positively glowing when Jessica was around.

Perhaps the crowning confirmation that Jessica was accepted had come from Grace

Talbot, his devoted, tight-lipped secretary, who, regally inclining her blue-tinted grey head, had paid Jessica what had been for her a fulsome compliment.

'Nurse Friday's a competent, efficient young woman who goes quietly about her business and keeps herself to herself.'

'Keeps herself to herself.' Oliver ran the words through his head. Was that a flaw in the otherwise perfect performance she gave each day? Why should it be if it didn't affect her work? What if she did keep herself to herself when off duty? That had absolutely nothing to do with him.

Of course it hadn't. He frowned and jingled the change in his trouser pocket. But had it something to do with Mrs Lowell-Smith's remark as he'd escorted her out of his consulting room? 'I like your Nurse Friday,' she'd said. 'Lovely manners, kind eyes…' Then she'd added after a minuscule pause. 'But so sad.'

Yes, that had been his impression at the interview, the sadness deep down in her kind, brown, gold-flecked eyes which contrasted so dramatically with the silver blonde hair.

He heard Jessica leave the examination room just as a BMW pulled into the drive. Mr

Jefferson no doubt. For the first time in years he had a moment's difficulty switching his mind away from the personal to the professional, but after that momentary hesitation he was back on line, firmly in professional mode.

He watched the man get out of his car. Sometimes that sort of preview of a patient gave him a valuable lead. Mr Jefferson was well dressed in a dark business suit. A compact sort of man, not very tall, and lean, as befitted a man who kept himself in trim. Yet surprisingly he walked with a slow, dragging step from his car to the front door.

Oliver strode across to his desk and picked up and reread the e-mail sent by Bob Cavendish, the man's previous GP.

Dear Oliver,
Roger Jefferson is a generally fit forty-year-old, a keen squash and golf player. Usually bounding with energy, he's recently complained of feeling exhausted, not being able to work well and having what he described as a bit of a bowel problem—occasional constipation. Have done an ECG, and heart, lungs, BP fine. He's near the top of his particular career ladder, something to do with

an up-market advertising agency, hence his move to Porthampton. I imagine a stressful sort of job. Hope you'll accept him on your private list and will do what you can to sort him out.

Yours, Bob

Forty, Oliver mused. I'm forty—nearly—and reasonably fit, though I don't have time for much golf or squash these days. And I suppose my job might be classed as stressful. But why is forty considered something special, a sort of benchmark in one's personal and professional life? Because it was a halfway mark in today's expected minimum life span?

A totally unexpected shiver of something akin to fear ran up his spine. *No!* Not fear, a premonition that something was very wrong indeed with the patient he was about to see. Based on what, he asked himself, a tired walk? Ludicrous! Yet the feeling persisted. He'd had similar sensations occasionally in the past, a kind of intuitive feeling that he was going to have to break especially bad news to a patient.

Breaking bad news, that was part of the job and he always found it hard, but some cases struck a particularly sensitive chord within him. He didn't dismiss the premonition as some medical colleagues might have done.

Long ago, a professor whom he'd admired had taught him the value of intuition. 'Use it, don't despise it,' he'd said. 'Ninety per cent of good diagnosis is instinct and intuition. Facts can sometimes be pretty thin on the ground.'

It took Oliver over half an hour to examine Mr Jefferson, literally from top to toe. Now he needed to think, before talking to the man. Superficially everything was ticking over fine, and yet... Had he felt the tip of something high up in the rectum, too high for his finger to reach? And why was there a slight, hardly noticeable yellow sheen on his skin? Perhaps the man was naturally sallow. There was no yellowing of the whites of his eyes, though his blue irises were cloudy, not the bright blue one might expect in a fit man of forty. So what did it all add up to?

He straightened to his full height and smiled down at his patient, who was eyeing him warily. 'I want you to stay put for the moment, Mr Jefferson. My nurse will be coming in to take some blood from you and do an ECG. We'll talk afterwards.'

The man frowned. 'But Bob Cavendish recently did an ECG and it was OK.'

'Nevertheless, I want another.' Oliver was firm.

Mr Jefferson looked resigned. 'Oh, well, you're the doctor,' he muttered wearily. 'But I hope it won't take long—I've got a lot to fit in today.'

Oliver injected a note of reassuring humour into his voice. 'As you say, I'm the doctor. Now, if you'd like to put on your trousers, but leave your shirt off, Nurse will be along in a couple of minutes.'

Back in his consulting room, he spoke to Jessica on the internal phone. 'Will you come through and take some blood from Mr Jefferson, Jessica? I've marked down what samples I want. And bring the ECG machine with you and do a readout for me, please. Also, will you do a before and after blood pressure. He'll probably complain that I've already done one and it's a waste of time doing another, but don't be deterred.'

Jessica gave a little snort. 'Certainly not, Doctor,' she said firmly.

It was a ladylike little snort, thought Oliver, smiling as he put down the phone, but a very determined one. His money was on Jessica. Jefferson was in a no-win situation.

He crossed to his favourite thinking spot by the window, staring out unseeingly. Bob Cavendish had been right—all the man's vital organs appeared to be fine. He had a great physique, certainly didn't *look* like a candidate for a heart problem. But at the prime age of forty there was no harm in making sure.

If it wasn't his heart, what was it that was making him so lethargic? Why the sallowness, the faint sheen of sweat? Except for what he described as occasional discomfort when he had his bowels open, he didn't complain of pain anywhere else. The manual examination of his rectum hadn't revealed anything obvious to cause discomfort. He ate sensibly, plenty of vegetables and fruit, drank tea and coffee sparingly. In fact, he was a model of healthy living.

So, what was wrong with the man?

Oliver punched the fist of his right hand into the palm of his left. Why did he have this gut feeling that something was badly wrong? One thing was for sure—he would arrange for a whole of battery of tests to be done at the Nightingale, starting with the use of a flexible fibre optic instrument to examine the higher reaches of the rectum and a biopsy if there was a hint of any irregularity. And he would have abdominal scans done to eliminate the possibility of irregularities in other organs.

At least the man could afford to be admitted to the clinic for two or three days and get the tests over in one fell swoop. Moneywise he could afford it, but would he be prepared to take time out of his business activities to have the tests? It was ironic that most of the patients at Arundel Street would have given their eye teeth to have received immediate treatment, but in Berkley Gardens... Here time was of the essence, affluence was earned at a price.

'No way,' said Roger Jefferson, his eyes angry and his jaw jutting out, when Oliver explained what needed to be done. 'I'll go in for a few hours for the examination, but I won't stay in. And I'll fit in another hour for the abdominal scan, but that's it. I don't know if you realise it, Dr Pendragon, but I'm just in the process of setting up new design studios here in Porthampton. I haven't time to go dragging my heels in a hospital bed—can't be done.'

He sounded belligerent and irritable as he stared at Oliver across the wide expanse of desktop. 'Look here, Bob gave you quite a build-up, said that if anyone could figure out what was wrong with me, you could. So why do you seem just as much at sea as he did? Why can't you give me something to buck me up?'

Oliver surveyed the angry man in silence for a moment. It was amazing how many even well-educated, informed people still seemed to think that a few tablets or something out of a bottle would cure them.

He said in a reasonable voice, 'On what you've told me, I can't make a diagnosis until I have more facts. These tests will provide some of those facts, either to confirm or eliminate a bowel problem, which is the only part of you that you admit is causing you discomfort.' He paused. 'Unless there's something you haven't told me, Mr Jefferson...' And there is, he thought, as the possibility took hold. The man's keeping something back, but what and why?

Why would he pay good money to seek help and not give me all the facts? Fear! said a small voice at the back of his head. The man's afraid of revealing something. He sat back in his chair, rested his chin on his clasped hands and waited...

Roger Jefferson remained silent for what seemed a long time, staring angrily back at Oliver. Then he slumped forward in his chair, screwed his forehead up into a frown and pressed his fingers against his temple. Fear and pain supplanted the anger in his eyes. His whole face screwed up. A sheen of sweat glistened on his taut cheeks, his lips were clamped into a thin line.

Oliver got up and moved swiftly round the desk. He poured some water from the carafe that stood on its polished top and held it to the man's lips. 'Drink,' he said firmly.

Mr Jefferson swallowed half a glassful of water almost greedily. He glanced up at Oliver. The pain in his eyes had dulled but the fear was still there. 'Thanks,' he murmured.

'Now,' said Oliver, 'tell me what's really wrong?'

The story came pouring out. The headaches that had started a few months before, mild at first, then getting increasingly severe. He'd put them down to stress. Even when he'd vomited on one occasion, he'd thought he'd been suffering from a migraine or sick headache. He'd swallowed an endless variety of over-the-counter products to relieve the symptoms. Some had worked better than others, but they all seemed to hold the worst of the pain at bay. Enough to let him keep on working.

'And that's when you began to have occasional constipation,' suggested Oliver.

'Yes.'

'Many pain relieving drugs cause constipation. Bob would have told you that had you explained that you were taking them by the bucketful.' He paused, and then asked gently, although he was pretty sure that he knew the answer, 'So why didn't you tell him about the headaches?'

Roger coloured beneath his sallow skin. 'I was scared to,' he admitted. 'I saw a programme on TV about...about brain tumours and...' He spread his hands helplessly.

'And wondered if you had—have—a tumour?'

'Yes.' He looked at Oliver with tired eyes. 'What do you think, Doctor? Have I a tumour or are these headaches caused by stress?'

'That I can't tell you, Mr Jefferson. It's something for a specialist to deal with, and the sooner the better. I'd like you return to the waiting room whilst I phone Professor Collins, a colleague of mine who's an eminent neurologist. I want you to see him as soon as possible. He's head of the neurology department at the University Hospital, but also sees patients privately. You couldn't be in better hands than his.'

That's true, Oliver mused a little later, having arranged an appointment for that afternoon for Jefferson to see Ben Collins, but if there is anything sinister going on, will we have got it in time? Why on earth had an educated man, who should have known better, let things go on the way he has? OK, so he was scared, but...

He puzzled over this on and off for the rest of the morning while dealing with another couple of patients, but couldn't find a satisfactory answer.

He saw his last patient out and listened to Jessica moving about in the examination room just as he had earlier in the day. Had she found out anything that might shed some light on the matter? He'd already had proof that patients often confided in her. Perhaps Mr Jefferson had let fall some interesting snippet of information. Such a snippet could be useful. He opened the door between the two rooms.

She had her back to the door and was collecting the instruments he had used for the last patient, ready to put into the steriliser. She obviously hadn't heard him enter.

Oliver watched her for a moment and found himself admiring the lithe, slim body, the wand-thin waist emphasised by the traditional wide belt—the trained nurse's emblem of office fastened by an elegant silver buckle.

He stood motionless in the doorway and stared, and found to his astonishment that he itched to span her waist with his hands. And hot on the heels of that desire the doctor in him wondered if she was not, in fact, a little too thin. He didn't go along with the school of thought which said that one couldn't be too thin—one could, and he'd seen enough instances of anorexia to know that the dividing line between fit and slim and unhealthily thin was a narrow one.

'Are you eating enough?' he asked brusquely, and wished the words back as he spoke.

Jessica spun round, a bunch of instruments in her hand, a startled expression on her face.

'Am I *what*?' she said, her voice incredulous.

There was no turning back. 'Eating enough,' Oliver repeated. 'I know it's fashionable to be slim, but...' He strove to extricate himself. Never was he at a loss for words. 'Look, what I mean is, being slim's fine, but not at the expense of not eating properly. You work hard and, rightly or wrongly, I feel responsible for my staff.'

Her eyebrows shot up, disappearing beneath her fringe, and her brown, gold-flecked eyes held a hint of amusement. Her lovely wide mouth curved into a smile.

'How very caring of you,' she said, her voice slightly husky.

'I try to be. I look out for my staff and they look out for my patients... So, are you eating enough?'

Jessica produced her lopsided smile and the dimple appeared. 'You sound like my mother,' she said. 'And, yes, I am eating enough. I lost some weight after the accident, but am fast regaining it. In fact, I've got a good appetite. I guess I'm one of the lucky few who can eat like the proverbial horse and not gain weight.'

Oliver nodded. 'Fair enough.' He cleared his throat. What had he come in for? Oh, yes, Jefferson. He said abruptly, 'Mr Jefferson. I've arranged for him to see Professor Collins...'

'The neurologist?'

'Yes...' He stared at her. Her face was wearing its usual calm expression. 'You don't seem surprised.'

'I'm not. He was so uptight I had a feeling he was hiding something, running scared. He didn't talk much, but when he did he couldn't seem to stop, and it was all about the pressure of work, as if that alone was responsible for his problems. I felt he was protesting too much and using work as a smokescreen.'

'Too right he is. How perceptive of you.'

Jessica read admiration in his piercing grey eyes. She coloured a little, strangely pleased with this scrap of praise.

She shrugged. 'Not really. I was going to mention it to you when I finished in here. After all, observation is part of a nurse's job—at least, that was what I was taught.'

'You had a good teacher.' He seemed interested, his tone of voice inviting more.

'Yes...an old-fashioned tutor when I did my practical. She was about to retire after seeing and not much liking the many changes in nurse training. I learned more from her, and from my mother who is a retired nurse, about real nursing than I did from textbooks. People need to be observed, cared for, reassured when they are ill, not just treated with drugs or procedures. Any trained technician can do that.'

She felt the colour rise higher in her cheeks as she spoke, and her breathing quicken. This was something she felt passionate about and she couldn't help it showing.

Oliver was astonished and delighted by this outburst. It was great to see her usual calm façade crack. He felt that he was privileged to see something of the real woman beneath the cool exterior. For a moment even the shadow of sadness had disappeared from her beautiful eyes. They were positively flashing amber. She was quite lovely.

He took a step toward her... His watch beeped urgently. 'Damn, I have a luncheon appointment.' He backstepped to the door. 'But we must continue this conversation some other time.'

A luncheon date. With beautiful, brainy Lucinda, Jessica guessed. 'And I must get on,' she said, gathering up the rest of the instruments from the trolley. 'I've a luncheon date, too.'

Oliver veiled his surprise and the faint feeling of annoyance that swept over him. *Who was she lunching with?* 'Then I musn't keep you—enjoy your lunch.' He nodded and disappeared through the door.

'Rachel and I usually do,' she murmured softly to his departing back. 'The local does a nice line in a ploughman's.'

CHAPTER FOUR

THE Fisherman's Arms, a black-beamed hostelry, discreetly tarted up without being brash, served the up-market clientele in the area. It was a fifteen-minute brisk walk, or a two-minute car journey, along the coast road from Berkley Gardens. It had a reputation for good bar food, and a high-class, pricey cuisine in the first-floor restaurant.

Jessica and Rachel went there most days for a pub lunch and a gossip.

It was as usual crowded, but a few minutes after they arrived a couple vacated a table by the log fire. Cradling their white wine spritzers, they fought their way round the packed bodies and took possession.

A moment later Rachel drawled, 'I say, don't look now, but look who's sailing up the stairs to the restaurant.'

Jessica did what everyone always did—turned her head and stared in the direction of the staircase. She was just in time to see Oliver, looking taller and broader than usual, following a diminutive blonde woman in a red velvet suit up the winding stairs. His hand was protectively on the small of her back. Both the cascading silky blonde hair and the blazing red of the suit were eye-catching and a dead give-away as to who she was, but it was the per-fection of the tiny figure that dispelled any doubt.

'It's Lucinda,' Jessica breathed, 'the Dresden-china blonde. You're dead right, Rachel, she's every man's dream of the fragile little woman, and he's...' Oliver turned his head at that moment and his grey eyes pierced the smoky distance between them and zoomed in on hers. Her spine tingled. She stared back for an instant, then bent her head over her drink. Had he really seen her or had she imag-ined it?

'Oliver's looking this way,' said Rachel. 'I believe he's seen us.' She lifted a hand in a languid wave.

Jessica shrugged. 'I shouldn't think so. He's too busy ogling Lucinda's neat little bottom.' Her voice, she heard in surprise, sounded brit-tle.

Rachel gave a toned-down hoot of laughter and gleamed a smile across at Jessica. 'Well, what did I tell you? Pretty and petite and preferably helpless, that's what all big men go for.'

'It's a well-known fact,' agreed Jessica dryly. 'But you also said that you thought the boss was immune, or at least not obviously mad about her, but right now he's looking every bit the large protective male.' Again the brittle edge.

'Would it bother you if he was?' Rachel's beautifully plucked brows lifted in a questioning fashion.

'Good Lord, it really hadn't crossed my mind. I've only known the man a few weeks.'

Rachel pulled a face. 'What's that got to do with it? You can fall for a guy at the drop of a hat... I do.'

Jessica smiled and leaned across the table to give Rachel's hand a squeeze. 'But you're a one-off,' she said, feeling a wave of affection for this elegant woman with a warm personality. They'd already formed a rapport and the plummy voice was no longer an irritant.

Later that day, knee deep in the babies' and toddlers' clinic at the Arundel Street surgery, Jessica recalled Rachel's words.

Did it bother her that Oliver might be seriously interested in Lucinda? And, if it did, for heaven's sake, why? She smothered the uncomfortable questions and called for the next infant.

'Peter Brown.' What a relief. After a succession of tongue twisting Bangledeshi or Indian names, nice, plain, English and easy to pronounce.

She smiled at the woman who was struggling with a wriggling baby as she picked her way round crawling toddlers and battered toys. The woman gave her a tired smile in return and laid the wide-eyed infant down on the table mat.

'Hello, poppet, you look bright and chirpy,' said Jessica, as she removed the baby's clothes, ready to weigh and examine him.

'You can say that again, Nurse,' said Peter's mother. There was a slight whine in her voice. 'Bright and chirpy describes him even at two o'clock in the morning. My husband's going spare. He needs his sleep, he has to get up early, and now that I've started back to work I need a bit of sleep, too.'

So what's a little lost sleep? Jessica felt like saying. He's fit and healthy and *alive*. She planted a kiss on the top of Peter's nearly bald little head. He beamed up at her, his eyes wide and very blue. Her treacherous heart skipped a painful beat. She gave him a quick hug and placed him on the scales.

'Just on thirteen pounds,' she said, automatically converting the kilogram reading. Even young women brought up on kilograms often preferred to have their baby's weight in old-fashioned pounds and ounces. She smiled across at Mrs Brown. 'That's bang on for four months, given his birthweight. Now, I'll have a listen to his chest and check his eyes and ears.'

Baby Peter gurgled and smiled as she ran her stethoscope over his tiny chest and Jessica pulled faces and made noises back at him. She was just pulling a particularly clownish face when the door at the end of the room opened and she looked up to see Oliver filling the doorway.

He stood for a moment just inside the door, laughing down at the noisy toddlers. Jessica registered that he had changed out of his consultant's gear into grey cords and a soft blue sweater. One two-year-old made an unsteady beeline for him, and he swooped her up into his arms and over his head so that she gurgled and chuckled with delight.

He looks great, so relaxed, informal, as though he's in his right element, thought Jessica. A ripple of pleasure ran through her as she straightened up and flashed a smile at him over the sea of toddlers. Meeting his eyes at a distance, it reminded her of the pub incident.

She felt her cheeks flushing and squashed the memory.

'Come to check up on me?' she asked as he came closer.

'Come to offer my services, if I can be of any help. They told me in Reception that you were inundated.' He looked round at the little black, brown and white faces. 'And they weren't kidding. We're short of cash, short of time, but one thing we're never short of here is kids.' His firm mouth tilted into a grin.

Jessica picked up baby Peter, dropped another kiss on his downy head and handed him over to Mrs Brown. 'He's fine,' she said. 'Tip-top condition. See you in a month's time or earlier if you're worried about anything.'

Half laughing, half serious, Mrs Brown said, 'You can't give him something to make him sleep at night, can you?' Her eyes swivelled from Jessica to Oliver. 'He's so damn lively.'

'No way,' they replied in unison.

'Just be happy that you've got a lovely healthy baby,' added Oliver, 'and treasure him.'

'Treasure him.' The words surprised Jessica, coming from Oliver, but, then, much surprised her as they worked side by side in the toddlers' clinic, not least his phenomenal memory for names.

Without glancing at the notes, he frequently reeled off the names of mums and babies and siblings, and remembered all kinds of details about them, often knowing where partners worked, or more often asking if they'd been lucky in getting a job. He quizzed the mums in the nicest possible way, finding out if they were in receipt of benefits they were entitled to and if promised repairs had been made to their houses or flats. Occasionally he made notes and promised to write letters on their be-half.

A young woman arrived as they were fin-ishing with their last patient. She had a three-year-old with her.

Oliver introduced mother and daughter to Jessica. 'This is Naomi,' he said, touching the little girl's dark curly head, 'and this is her mum, Mrs Gloria Walker.' Mrs Walker, a proud, handsome-looking Jamaican woman, was heavily pregnant. 'Naomi in the wars again?' he asked her.

'Yes, Doctor, she just fall down the kitchen steps and hollered and said her wrist hurt, though she ain't cryin' now, but I brought her in just like you said.'

Oliver nodded. 'Quite right.' Lifting the toddler up onto the table, he explained to Jessica, 'Naomi is inclined to be accident-prone, and, though not officially classed as having brittle bone disease, she has had several fractures and she bruises easily so we like to keep an eye on her if she has a fall.'

Was this code for, We're not sure if these are accidents or due to parental abuse or neglect?

Reading her mind, Oliver demolished the idea as he gently examined Naomi's wrist.

'It happened once when I was in the house, visiting Mr and Mrs Walker senior. They live with Gloria and her husband, George, and are both elderly and frail. Naomi tumbled off a low chair and fractured her clavicle. It happened like that.' He snapped his fingers, then laid a hand for an instant on Mrs Walker's shoulder. 'And Gloria here looks after them all. George does what he can when he's home, but he's a long-distance lorry driver and is frequently away for days at a time.'

It was a perfect testimonial to the Walkers as a loving, caring couple.

Jessica felt humble. She smiled at Gloria. A toddler, a baby on the way and her in-laws to care for. 'Good Lord, how on earth do you manage, especially with your husband being away so much? It must be difficult for you.'

Gloria smiled broadly, showing gleaming white teeth against her dark skin. It was natural, quite different to Rachel's toothpaste smile. 'Difficult! Not so difficult when most of our neighbours haven't got no jobs at all. We're lucky, George and me, and the old 'uns aren't much trouble, and they're great with this one here.' She ruffled Naomi's hair.

What a difference to Peter's mum, the whiny Mrs Brown.

Oliver had finished examining the toddler's hand and arm. 'I'm pretty sure it's not broken, just sprained,' he told Gloria. 'Naomi's got full finger movement without much pain, but we'll put on a special hand-to-elbow plastic support cast to make sure she doesn't use it for a week or so. Obviously you must bring her back if she complains of more severe pain, otherwise make an appointment to see me in a fortnight's time and I'll check it then.'

Little Naomi watched with dark luminous eyes as Jessica supported her tiny hand and arm and Oliver applied the padded plastic splint.

'There you are, love,' he said, when he'd finished. 'Now, what about a sweetie for an extra-good girl?' He lifted the sweetie tin down from the shelf and made a production out of opening it.

'What do you say, Naomi?' asked her mother.

'Pleeth,' said Naomi, bouncing up and down and holding out a little chubby paw.

'So, what colour are we going to have?' Oliver tilted the tin of gaily wrapped sweets low enough for the little girl to look into. The plump fingers wavered for a moment, then swooped in and drew out a purple lollipop.

'What do you say?' Gloria prompted again.

Naomi hung her head, suddenly shy. 'Fank you,' she whispered.

'Thank you, Doctor, and you, Nurse.' Gloria inclined her head graciously, reminding Jessica of the gracious bow that the white haired Mrs Lowell-Smith had given them that morning. Poles apart in culture, one poor and one rich, yet there was a similarity between the two women. Good manners came naturally to both of them.

'What a lovely woman,' said Jessica, when mother and daughter had departed minutes later.

'Yes, it's a pleasure to care for her and her family, makes up for the moaners in both practices. Mind you, some of them have plenty to moan about, living on subsistence handouts in crummy bedsits or worse. But it certainly sorts out the wheat from the chaff.'

'Yes, most of them are amazingly cheerful, considering the way life's treated them. There were even a couple of dads here with their babies because their wives were working, and they seemed to take it in their stride. There's something particularly touching about a man being gentle with a baby.'

Now why had she said that? Be-cause…because… Jessica bent and tidied away toys into the box to hide her confusion and the tears stinging the backs of her eyes. When she stood up a few moments later she'd recovered her cool. She stretched, and shafted a quick glance at Oliver. 'Thanks so much for your help. I wouldn't be finished yet if it weren't for you.'

'Always glad of an excuse to work with the mums and babies—makes up for the seamier side of the job.' Oliver glanced at his watch, not the gold Rolex he wore in Berkley Gardens but a plain one on a leather strap. He looked up at Jessica. 'It's a long time since lunch. Are you hungry?'

Was he reminding her of lunchtime in the pub and the look? So what? She nodded. 'Starving and thirsty. The kids make for hot work. I could drink gallons of tea. I've just about finished here so I'll pop along to the staffroom, before going home. What about you? Can I make you a cup of something?'

'I've got a better idea. I've an hour to go before evening surgery. If you're not in a rush to get away, we could go to Frank's Fodder and get the best cup of tea in town—you know, the sort you can stand your spoon up in. He also does the best fry-up, mixed grill, call it what you will, for miles around—bacon, sausage, egg, chips, tomatoes, mushrooms and anything else Frank can think to throw in.'

Jessica's eyebrows shot up. 'I'd never have put you down as a strong tea man. You usually drink Earl Grey with lemon.'

Oliver shrugged. 'In Berkley Gardens...when in Rome, you know... And I enjoy it, but on a cold autumn day like today, I prefer the sort of tea that my mother makes, good and hot and strong. God knows what it does to the stomach, but it's certainly got body in it and gives one a nice kick.'

In the nick of time Jessica stopped her eyebrows shooting up again and clamped her mouth shut on the exclamation of surprise that rose to her lips. The sort of tea his mother makes! His mother? So his mother was still alive—not that there was any reason that she shouldn't be. He was only fortyish, so she could easily be as young as sixty. But surely she would be a grand, gracious lady rather like Mrs Lowell-Smith, and would have someone around to make dainty cups of tea for her. Yet the doctor made her sound like a homely little woman wearing a pinny and pottering around a tiny kitchen.

'Well, are you ready to do justice to a decent cup of tea and a nice, solid meal at Frank's?' Oliver's grey eyes, softened by the blue of his sweater, had lost their steeliness and almost twinkled. 'You told me this morning that you could eat anything without putting on a gram. I'd like to see you tuck into Frank's fry-up.'

Was that only this morning, Jessica thought, when he'd remarked on her thinness? And what about Lucinda? Would she mind that the doctor who, according to Rachel, she considered *hers*, was taking his practice nurse out for tea—even if it was to the least likely venue for a romantic interlude? Frank's Fodder, a pull-in for lorry drivers. Surely nowhere could be less romantic.

A picture of the arrogant head and irritating tight little bottom of the Dresden-china figure disappearing up the stairs in the pub flashed into her mind. So what? She isn't here to object, and it's time I got to know the man.

Jessica said happily, 'I'd love to sample Frank's lethal fry-up. Just give me a minute to fetch my coat.'

*   *   *

A quarter of an hour later, Frank himself was placing a monster pot of tea in front of them.

'Long time no see, Doc,' he said. 'You're a sight for sore eyes.' He nodded a smile at Jessica as he unloaded a milk jug, sugar basin and cutlery onto the table.

'Miss Friday's our practice nurse,' Oliver explained.

'I suppose 'e's bin runnin' 'imself into the ground as usual,' Frank said with another nod at Jessica.

Oliver grinned. 'I can speak for myself, thank you. I've been keeping busy enough, Frank. How's the family?'

'They're all bloomin', thanks, Doc. Ain't 'ad no call for your services.'

'I'm glad to hear it.' Oliver turned to Jessica. 'Frank's got twin boys of eighteen months.'

'But I wouldn't 'ave if it weren't for the doc 'ere. They came in an 'ell of a rush and 'e delivered 'em upstairs, and one 'ad the cord round 'is neck, and wouldn't 'ave made it if it 'adn't been for the doc.'

To Jessica's delight, Oliver blushed slightly. 'Any good midwife could have done the same, Frank. I just happened to be available.'

Jessica slanted a sly smile at him. 'But home deliveries can be tricky,' she said, 'especially when it's twins.'

'Right on,' said Frank, 'but the doc 'ere didn't turn a hair.'

Embarrassed by Frank's adulation, he was turning more than a hair now. Jessica took pity on him. She looked at Frank. 'Your wife didn't bring them to the toddlers' clinic this afternoon.'

'No, she's away with 'er mum for a few days.'

'I look forward to meeting her and the boys at our next clinic.'

'I'll tell 'er. Now, what can I get you folks?'

'Your biggest and best fry-up, Frank, please.'

'You got it.'

He disappeared back behind the counter, and Oliver said, 'Shall I pour or will you?'

All at once his voice was soft, almost seductive, his eyes caressing, as if he was speaking of something else.

Her cheeks flamed and her pulses leapt. She took a diaphragm-deep breath and eyed the outsize teapot. 'What, with that thing full of tea? Thanks, but I'm not looking for a sprained wrist.'

Oliver poured the rich amber liquid into their breakfast-sized mugs. Then he picked up his and held it aloft. 'To a successful working partnership,' he said. 'And may it continue as well as it has started.'

His deep voice was warm, reassuring. Jessica glowed. She raised her mug and clicked it against his. 'I second that,' she said.

Food on huge plates, colourful, steamy and aromatic, arrived a few minutes later and they both fell on it eagerly.

They ate in silence for several minutes, then Jessica paused and sat back in her chair. 'You were right—it's absolutely delicious,' she said. 'But definitely a once-in-a-blue-moon treat. I can almost feel my cardiac arteries gunging up.'

'Actually,' replied Oliver, 'it's more grilled and oven-cooked than fried, but Frank's Fry-Up sounds more substantial fodder for some of the hefty drivers who patronise him. Now, tell me, apart from the practice, how are you settling down in Porthampton? We never seem to have much time for personal exchanges at either surgery. Are you still living at the guest house?' His intensely blue-grey eyes searched hers.

'Yes, but only until Saturday. I'm very lucky, I've got a long lease on a little cottage on the Spit—it's the end of a terrace of what were once fishermen's cottages. I move in at the weekend. It's unfurnished, which is just what I want. The stuff from my London flat has been stored in Devon since the accident, and it'll be great to have my own things around me again.'

She realised that for the first time she had referred to the accident without gagging on the word. Please, God, let it mean that the pain was beginning to dull just a little. It would never go, she wouldn't want it to, the memories were too precious, but...

Oliver watched her cheeks pale and a shadow cross her face and, unusually for him, said the first thing that came into his head, anything to take that look off her face. 'You're going to be busy. Do you want a hand moving in?' His voice was casual. 'I ask because, except for a visit to the Nightingale, I've nothing organised for the weekend. Might as well be doing something useful. Unless, of course, you've help planned...'

Jessica stared at him across the narrow table. Had she heard right? Did he mean it? Why say it if he didn't? She said breathily, 'Only what the removal men give me, and I dare say on a Saturday they'll be itching to get off to football or something. My parents would have come up from Devon, but they've a long-standing obligation to meet.'

Good God, that made her sound lonely and pathetic. She forced a smile to her lips. 'Rachel said she might look in, but that will depend on—'

'Her tame dental surgeon.' Oliver grinned. 'Looks as if I'm your only option,' he said. He took another forkful of food and chewed it appreciatively. 'So what time shall I report on duty?'

He was going too fast for her. The idea of Oliver Pendragon, her distinguished boss, shifting her furniture around was mind-boggling. And what about Lucinda? How would she react to him giving up part of his precious off duty to help another woman? Her body language at the pub, the confident way she had wiggled her buttocks, had spoken volumes.

Anyway, Jessica wasn't sure that *she* wanted this man sitting opposite her, literally throwing his weight and personality about in her little cottage. She meant to make it her own, not share it with anyone. She pulled herself up short. Good Lord, the man was only offering a bit of muscle, and beneath that leanness he had plenty of that. As for Lucinda, she was more than capable of looking after herself, and if she wasn't—tough.

This time she smiled more easily. 'Thank you, Dr Pendragon, I'll take you up on your offer. My furniture should arrive about ten, so any time after then would be great.'

Oliver was surprised by the wave of pleasure that surged through him—partly because he found the idea of getting to know this cool, detached woman strangely exciting, partly because he had succeeded in wiping that guarded, desolate expression from her face, so clearly associated with the accident that had taken her out of circulation for over a year. Perhaps one day she might confide in him...

He said, 'Good, I'm glad that's settled.' He took another forkful of food, but paused with it halfway to his mouth. 'There's just one condition about Saturday...'

She knew a moment's unease. 'And that is?'

'That we drop the "doctor" bit. It's Oliver when we're off duty—agreed?'

'Agreed.'

Driving back to the guest house a little later, her mind buzzed with all sorts of sensations. It had been a strange day from the moment that Oliver had asked her if she ate enough. Such an extraordinary personal remark for the usually aloof doctor to make, and in such a tender tone—as if he really cared.

Work never being far from her mind, the memory triggered thoughts about Roger Jefferson. What had been the result of his scan? Did he have a cerebral tumour, poor man? Thank goodness Oliver had sensed, as she had, that something was seriously wrong, and had continued to probe. A lesser doctor might have given up—but no way could Oliver Pendragon be called a lesser doctor.

In the short while she had worked for him, she had discovered that he was held in great respect at both the private and NHS hospitals. And it was obvious that he was liked and admired in both surgeries. And this was the man who was going to heave her furniture around

on Saturday! She wasn't sure that she under-
stood why he had offered. Neither was she
sure why she had accepted...unless in some
obscure way it had something to do with the
luscious Lucinda!

Lucinda! The little woman who seemed to
hold her distinguished, confident boss in thrall.
Or did she? Was it only a superficial hold, or
was it the big-man-helpless-little-woman syn-
drome from which even Oliver Pendragon, sophisticated man of the world, wasn't immune?

Or was it something much simpler than
that? Did the fact that Lucinda was the daughter of Lady Grant, the local society hostess
with an enormous amount of clout, have anything to do with it? Jessica gave a little snort
of disgust. No, of course it didn't. She didn't
know the man well, but well enough to be sure
that on a personal level he was no social
climber.

Anyway, he didn't need to be—he was distinguished enough on his own account. But
Lady Grant was a superb fund-raiser, and
Rachel had hinted that he was always in the
market for projects at the Arundel Street surgery. Was he, in fact, leading Lucinda, rather
being led by her? Going along with her to keep

in favour with her mother? She frowned. That didn't sound very honourable, rather sleazy, in fact.

So maybe Rachel had got it wrong. Perhaps Oliver was genuinely attracted to her. Maybe beneath that brittle little doll-like exterior, which, according to Rachel, reflected a selfish interior, she was a soft and gentle woman. She would try to keep an open mind until she met her and could judge for herself, whenever that might be.

CHAPTER FIVE

JESSICA came face to face with Lucinda Grant the next afternoon in Reception. Perched on the corner of the elegant gilt desk and swinging an equally elegant leg, she was deep in what seemed an almost furtive conversation with Rachel. Rachel was looking ruffled, not in the least her languid laid-back self.

Crossing the wide, richly carpeted expanse from the door, Jessica noted that though Lucinda might be tiny, she had a lot of long, curvy leg and was busy displaying it. And what ankles! Their slenderness was enhanced by stiletto-heeled, strappy sandals and high, arching insteps. Her own were slim, but these... Oliver could have circled them easily with his long fingers.

She found the idea distasteful. Physically he was an attractive man, though she wasn't sure that he was her type. He was too aloof at times. So why did it bother her? Because they'd worked harmoniously together with the toddlers and he was so genuine? Or because they

had seemed so close, sharing a fry-up at
Frank's Fodder? The thought of Lucinda hob-
nobbing with Frank was laughable.

She strangled the thought and murmured,
'Good afternoon.' Lucinda ignored the greet-
ing, and stared at her with cold violet-blue
eyes.

Rachel seemed struck dumb and made no
attempt at an introduction, but her eyes sig-
nalled that she was pleased and relieved to see
Jessica.

Jessica spoke directly to her. 'Will you
make another appointment for Mrs Bell for
next week, please, Rachel? And will you order
a taxi? She'll be ready to leave soon.'

Rachel smiled. 'With pleasure.' She riffled
through the appointment book. 'Would two
o'clock next Thursday be OK?'

'Fine.' Jessica took the embossed appointment card Rachel had filled in, and with a nod
toward Lucinda turned to leave.

Lucinda slid off the desk and stood in front
of her, barring her way. Even with her heels,
she barely came up to Jessica's shoulder, making her feel a clumsy giant. 'And you can tell
Oliver that I'm here and must see him,' she
said in an imperious high voice. 'You know

who I am, of course...' Witheringly, the cold eyes swept over Jessica from top to toe.

Jessica itched to slap the porcelain face and was tempted to say that she didn't know her, but decided not to stoop to such childishness. Lucinda was nauseatingly confident that she was a focus of interest who would have been discussed and described. And she was dead right.

'I do, Miss Grant.' She kept her cool and her voice professional. 'But I don't know if Dr Pendragon will be able to see you at once. He has several important phone calls to make before his next patient.'

Lucinda tossed her head and her long hair rippled. 'Oh, he'll see me. Just tell him that I'm here.'

'I'll tell him,' Jessica said, her voice and eyes icy as she looked down on the spoilt, rude creature in front of her. How on earth did Oliver tolerate her? 'Now, please, let me pass, Miss Grant, I've a patient waiting.'

Lucinda stepped aside with a snort.

Fuming over idle rich bitches, until she remembered that Lucinda was rich but not idle— in fact, she was a computer expert—Jessica returned to the consulting room.

'All fixed, Nurse?' Oliver gave her his usual polite, professional smile that he kept for Berkley Gardens in front of patients.

So much at variance with his Arundel Street smile, Jessica thought. He was equally kind and caring with all his patients, whatever their status, but there were subtleties of difference in the way he talked to each group of people. The phrase 'all things to all men' popped into her mind. Was he that, or just a very good actor, a fashionable doctor who knew where his bread was buttered—and jammed?

The memory resurfaced of the man who had drunk strong tea and demolished an enormous fry-up in Frank's Fodder...the man who had offered to help her move. She dismissed the idea of him acting a part.

Her smile was as professional as his. 'All fixed, Doctor. There we are, Mrs Bell.' She handed over the appointment card. 'Your next appointment, and Rachel is phoning for a taxi.' She smiled down at the elderly, fragile little lady. 'Now, Mrs Bell, may I give you an arm?'

'Well, thank you, dear.' Mrs Bell said her goodbyes to Oliver as he stood to shake her hand.

'I'll see you to the—' he began.

Mrs Bell shook her head. 'There's no need,' she said. 'You're a busy man—you get on with your work. Nurse will take care of me.' She slipped her arm into Jessica's and squeezed her forearm. 'Slim, but nice and firm,' she murmured with a sigh. 'What I wouldn't do to be young and strong again, my dear. I know it's a corny thing to say, but you're only young once so make the most of it—live life to the full.'

Make the most of it! Live life to the full! Jessica tried to stem the wave of familiar bleakness that suddenly engulfed her. Live life to the full when...

Abruptly, tears burned at the back of her eyes. Somehow she scrambled together a smile of sorts and beamed it down to the old lady.

'How right you are, Mrs Bell,' she said cheerfully.

At the door she turned and spoke to Oliver, glad of the width of the room between them. She might have deceived Mrs Bell but he would notice the glitter in her eyes. 'By the way, Doctor, Miss Grant is waiting to see you. Shall I ask her to come in?' Moment of truth. Would he agree to see her immediately, as Lucinda was so sure he would?

He picked up the phone and held the receiver to his ear. 'Please, tell Miss Grant that I'm on the phone, Nurse, and I have a patient booked in in fifteen minutes. If she cares to wait till after I've seen that patient...'

His grey eyes, speaking volumes, held Jessica's across the room. Phrase that as you will, they seemed to say, whilst his voice said politely but firmly that Lucinda could take it or leave it.

Great! Jessica's spirits lifted a little—she wasn't sure why, but she would have hated him to have meekly given in. Childish or not, it would give her enormous pleasure to relay his message to the smug doll-like creature in Reception.

Trying to keep the jubilation out of her voice, she said brightly, 'Certainly Doctor.' Making polite conversation with Mrs Bell, she escorted her out to wait for her car.

'He said *what*?' exploded Lucinda a minute later. 'I don't believe it.' Pushing roughly past Jessica and Mrs Bell, she tore along the corridor to the consulting room.

Feeling Mrs Bell tremble, Jessica put a protective arm round her waist, led her over to an armchair and seated her gently.

Mrs Bell murmured, looking from Jessica to Rachel, 'What a rude young woman.'

Jessica would have liked to have heartily endorsed the statement, but in the interests of practice politics she simply apologised. 'I'm so sorry about that, Mrs Bell. She'd been waiting rather a long time and was very anxious to see Dr Pendragon.' She tried to imply that it was an urgent health matter which might have excused the rude behaviour.

Mrs Bell wasn't impressed. She sighed sadly. 'In my day, manners meant something. Nobody seems to care these days—no manners, no respect. I just hate the way the world's going. Glad that I'll be leaving it soon.'

And that, thought Jessica, knowing that the elderly woman was slowly losing a long battle with pernicious anaemia, could be on the cards any moment.

She crouched down and took the cold, paper-thin hands in her own. 'What you need, Mrs Bell, is a hot drink. Tea, coffee?'

Rachel shot out of her chair and crossed to a side table where coffee percolated fragrantly and a glass kettle was kept at the ready for making tea. 'What's your poison, Mrs Bell?'

she asked, clearly happy to do something for the old lady in the face of Lucinda's rudeness.

The elderly lady smiled a bit shakily. 'What I need is a stiff dry Martini, heavy on the gin, with lots of ice and lemon,' she said.

Rachel raised her hands in mock despair. 'So sorry, we're right out of gin at the moment.'

The bantering reply pleased Mrs Bell. 'Oh, well, in that case, since beggars can't be choosers, it'll have to be coffee, hot, black and sweet, please.'

'Coming up.' Rachel beamed.

It was at that moment that Lucinda, her face registering fury, erupted back into Reception. Without uttering a word, she swept across the room and out into the vestibule.

Mrs Bell raised thinning eyebrows. 'Ah, so that's the way of it—a lover's tiff.' She shook her head. 'Not that she'll get far with Dr Pendragon till she mends her manners. *He's* too much of a gentleman to tolerate such behaviour.' She looked brightly from Jessica to Rachel, too polite to ask directly but obviously hoping for a clue as to what was going on.

Jessica tried to think of something innocuous to say that wouldn't embarrass Oliver, or make the old lady feel uncomfortable. She was still searching for the right words when Rachel placed a cup of steaming coffee on the small table beside Mrs Bell's chair. 'There we go. Sorry it's not a Martini, but it's hot, black and sweet as ordered.'

'Thank you, my dear.' The faded but shrewd eyes twinkled. 'That's as neat a way as any to tell me to mind my own business. And quite right, too, to protect your employer's privacy. I commend you both for that. I shouldn't have tried to pry, put it down to old age and a genuine affection for the doctor. He's a good man and deserves only the best.' She sipped her coffee. 'That's lovely, just as I like it.' And with a smile and a nod she dismissed the episode as if it had never happened.

'He's a good man and deserves only the best.' And 'he's too much of a gentleman' and she won't 'get far with Dr Pendragon till she mends her manners'.

Mrs Bell's words circled round in Jessica's head as she went about her chores over the course of the next couple of days. She wasn't the first patient to express those or similar sentiments. He was quite simply a man who was generally liked and admired...and trusted.

Trusted! Quite suddenly, the desire to tell him all about her accident was overwhelming.

She tried to banish the thought. Normally she was able to set aside personal affairs when on duty, but this time she found it difficult. Alone in the treatment room, testing urine samples and squirting blood into vials, she mulled over the idea.

They were routine jobs and letting her mind wander didn't matter, but she was disgusted with herself when, in the middle of the weight watchers' clinic, a vivid image of the predatory Lucinda flashed into her mind.

It hit her as she was charting the tiny amount of weight gained by an almost anorexic teenager. Her pen shook. It took a moment to find her voice. 'Well done, Tracy, you've gained nearly two hundred and twenty five grams. That's great.'

'What's that in old money, Nurse?' asked Tracy's mother.

'Nearly half a pound,' said Jessica.

'I must be getting better, Nurse musn't I?' said Tracy, her thin face transformed by a warm smile.

'You certainly are, Tracy,' confirmed Jessica. 'Keep up the good work, love. See you next week.'

Her next patient, Betty Snow, had a problem at the other end of the scale. She needed assurance that to have lost a couple of pounds in a week was good going.

'I could do better,' the ample Betty was saying, 'if I didn't have to cook all those meals for the boys. They expect hot midday dinners and another one in the evening. By the time I've cleared up I'm whacked, and just eat up the leftovers.'

By concentrating hard, Jessica tuned in to what Betty Snow was saying. The 'boys' meant her husband and two strapping great teenage sons. They worked in the docks and the sons played football for the local amateur team.

'Then you deserve a medal for losing anything, Betty. And no wonder you're whacked out, what with all that washing and ironing.' She shuddered. 'I don't know how you do it. And you work in the pub some nights, don't you?'

'Yeah, well, I need to, in spite of what they earn.' Betty shrugged. 'Everything costs. But to tell you the truth, Nurse, I'm glad to get out of the house and meet a few other faces. It keeps me from going round the bend.'

'I can imagine.' She smiled at the nicely made-up woman with her still pretty face. 'You know, Betty, you should be as thin as a pin the way you work.'

Betty shrugged again. 'Well, there you go. My dear mum was fat, and she worked all hours God sent until the day she died. But I'm going to beat this thing if it kills me. Goodbye, Nurse, see you next week. Thanks for everything.'

For what? Jessica mused. All I did was weigh her and take her blood pressure—she's done all the hard work. It's just not fair that people who can afford it in time or money can lose pounds by doing a workout. Betty fitted the stereotypical pattern of so many older working women, waiting on their families at their own expense. The modern approach to marriage seemed to have passed them by.

'Perhaps you're right, Dad,' she said to the empty room. 'Perhaps there is too much emphasis on thinness and fitness being linked together. Except for being overweight, Betty's as fit as a flea. Maybe—'

'Maybe what?' asked Oliver from the door. 'I did knock,' he added. 'Thought you said to come in.'

'Oh.' Jessica jumped. 'Sorry about that, I was thinking out loud.'

Oliver crossed the room. 'Thoughts you can share, or shouldn't I ask?'

Jessica gaped. What thoughts was he alluding to? Her Betty thoughts or her Lucinda thoughts? Blood rushed to her cheeks and then receded. Fool! He doesn't know what your thoughts were. They're in your head.

She stopped gaping. 'Oh, quite sharable ones,' she said, her voice cool. 'I was recalling my father's theory.'

'And his theory is?'

'That you don't necessarily *have* to be thin to be fit—it's possible to be fat and fit, and he has plenty of patients on his list to prove it.'

Oliver perched one buttock on the bench. He compressed his thin but well-marked lips for a moment, and looked thoughtfully at Jessica.

'Yes, I think I go along with that. Not grossly overweight people, of course—they usually are running into trouble. But there are some people who are better for carrying a little extra weight. It suits them and they're certainly happier.'

'The guilt factor, that's what Dad calls this obsession with dieting, leading to depression. People feel guilty about being fat, poor, under-achievers—anything that doesn't fit in with what our masters, whoever they are, think is right for us.' Jessica shuffled her stool a few inches away from Oliver's long, swinging leg.

'Well, depressive illness is certainly on the increase. Your father could be right.' He slanted her a smile and slid from the bench. 'But I'm holding you up—you've several more people to see. I'm off now, I just wanted to confirm what time you want me to report for duty tomorrow.'

'Tomorrow?' Jessica said blankly, her mind still on the warmth of his leg moments before. 'Duty?'

'You're moving house, remember? And I offered my services.' He frowned and pulled a long face. 'Oh, dear, my delicate ego's flat-tened. You've forgotten.'

Jessica gave an uncertain little laugh. Memory flooded back. They'd said ten, hadn't they? She tut-tutted. 'Now, would I forget such an offer? Any time after ten, that's if you're sure.'

He said with quiet emphasis, 'I'm sure, but the address? It's in the row of fishermen's cottages on the Spit, I know, but which one?'

'Number six—right at the end of the row, almost in the sea.'

'Till tomorrow at ten—let's hope the weather holds fine.'

'Weatherwise, my hopes are dashed,' Oliver said cheerfully, when he arrived soon after ten on Saturday morning. He dodged the removal men, who were heaving furniture and packing cases through the door, and, striding through the tiny hall separating the living room from the front door, made for the kitchen.

Had he been here before? wondered Jessica, following him through. He seemed to know his way. She grinned foolishly at his wet, raincoated back—not that there was much chance of missing it. There wasn't anywhere else to go from the hall, unless it was up the stairs.

Oliver plonked several plastic carriers down on the table.

Oliver Pendragon and plastic bags shouldn't go together, thought Jessica, but they did this morning. Perhaps it was the wet mac. Or was it a trench coat? it looked vaguely military, squaring his already broad shoulders.

'I come with goodies, but I see that I should have got here earlier.' He waved his hand at the used teamugs and opened packets of biscuits.

Rain was bucketing down, wind was beating against the windows, and green waves with curling white tops were crashing on the shoreline a few hundred yards away. By contrast, the warm kitchen seemed an oasis of quiet.

Jessica blinked at this new, different Oliver, who belonged neither to Berkley Gardens nor to Arundel Street.

'Where can I hang this?' he asked, shrugging off his raincoat, and looking round for a likely hook.

Jessica struggled to clear her throat which had suddenly dried up.

He opened the garden door. 'Ah, thought there'd be a porch and hooks—there usually are in these sorts of cottages.'

These sorts of cottages. What did he know about these sorts of cottages?

He was wearing jeans and a creamy thick knit sweater and chunky trainers. He looked…

She took a deep breath—she hadn't imagined those long, muscular legs in jeans.

She moistened her lips and found her voice. 'The men got here earlier than I expected. Apparently they came up from Devon yesterday, delivering furniture *en route*, and stayed in Porthampton overnight. They should be finished soon. The guest house was marvellous, they gave me flasks of tea and biscuits to be going on with.'

'Good,' said Oliver. 'When they go, we can really get cracking.' He pushed up the sleeves of his sweater in a workmanlike fashion, revealing a scattering of dark hairs on his forearms.

On cue, the foreman put his head round the door. 'We're all finished, so we'll be off.'

Bemused by this new breezy Oliver, unpacking bags, Jessica said faintly, 'Do you want more tea before you go?'

'No, thanks, we want to get back for the match this afternoon. Starts at three—traffic permitting, we should just make it.'

Jessica handed him an envelope. 'If you'll share that out, please. Thanks for your help, you've been great.'

She followed him through to the front door and closed it behind him, then rested her back against the sturdy white-painted panels and took a few steadying breaths. It was quiet, except for noises coming from the kitchen—the clink of china, the sound of water running—and then the heavenly scent of fresh coffee.

Coffee, wonderful! Picking her way round packing cases, she tiptoed through the living room and stood in the kitchen doorway, watching Oliver. He was at the sink, washing up the dirty mugs. A coffee percolator was plugged into a socket above the work bench and was just beginning to bubble.

What was this tall, dark, alien man doing in her humble kitchen, washing up as if he had done it all his life? The Berkley Square man had a housekeeper to do that for him in his flat above the consulting rooms.

Mrs Lemon wouldn't let him lift a cup. 'He works far too hard,' she'd told Jessica only a few days ago, when they'd met by the staff entrance. 'He needs a good, loving wife to look after him, but he's leaving it a bit late to find the right one.'

Had that meant that she didn't consider Lucinda the right one? Presumably. Sensible and down to earth, she would have seen through luscious Lucinda in a flash.

'Not that it matters one jot to me,' Jessica had muttered, as she'd crossed the drive to her car. 'If he wants to make a fool of himself with a nasty piece of work like Lucinda, that's his affair.'

Now she stared at the wide shoulders and dark head of her employer, bent over her sink, and marvelled. What *was* he doing here, using his precious free time to help her? And with such a mundane task?

Even at Arundel Street, which was a madhouse, the receptionists kept him supplied with coffee, and she'd certainly never seen him elbow deep in soapy water. Yet here he was in her newly acquired little home, looking at ease and domesticated as to the manner born. That rarity, a truly modern man, willing to share chores with his partner.

Partner! She almost choked on the thought, and he turned and smiled at her, a wide, tender smile. *Tender?* No, she couldn't mean tender. Gentle, perhaps—the sort of smile he gave patients to reassure them.

Huh, she didn't need reassuring.

'Come and sit down and have some decent coffee,' he said, beckoning her in. 'I part percolated it before leaving home so it'll be ready in minutes.' He pulled out an old-fashioned wooden chair.

As if it's *his* kitchen, not mine, she thought. How arrogant could you get? She opened her mouth to give some smart retort—but her mind was empty. She sat down. 'Yes, oh, Master,' she said with pretended meekness.

Oliver grinned and his eyes glinted. 'You like being your own woman, don't you, Jessica?'

Jessica bristled. 'Is there anything wrong in that?'

'Nothing. I like strong-minded women.'

Perhaps that explained Lucinda—or was she strong-willed rather than strong-minded, like a wilful child? No, she had to be tough to have reached the top in the competitive computer world. So was he drawn to competitive women? Was that Lucinda's attraction, a strong enough attraction to overlook her rudeness?

Her thoughts slid sideways. Would he consider me competitive? she wondered. She almost shrugged. Why should he? She was the only nurse on the team, there was no one to compete with. Though she had been competitive, a long time ago. The youngest ward sister in her hospital with her career all mapped out before her. That was until—

She jumped as Oliver pushed a fragrant mug of coffee, as well as demerara sugar and cream, across the table. 'You're in what my mother would call a brown study,' he said softly.

Jessica pressed her cheeks in a fruitless attempt to stop herself from blushing. 'I'm so sorry. How rude of me. I—I was just…'

'Deep in thought. About what, Jess, or shouldn't I ask?'

Rain and wind lashed against the small casement window. Jess—he'd called her Jess. She stared into his eyes through the steam spiralling upwards from their mugs.

Perhaps it was the steam, hanging like a veil between them, or the gentleness in his voice, or the feeling that they were cut off from the world on this finger of land thrusting out into the raging sea, but suddenly she felt bold, wanted to talk, to ask questions. He was always asking her questions, so why shouldn't she ask him?

'Why Lucinda?' The words just spurted out.

Oliver's eyebrows shot up. His eyes flared with amusement...or was it surprise at her boldness? He sipped at his coffee. 'What do you mean, why Lucinda?'

Jessica stared down into the dark aromatic depths of her mug. Why *had* that particular question popped out of her mouth, and how to explain it? Tell the truth? Say, because I want to know why a clever, kind, caring man like you is attracted to a spoilt creature like her, even if she is a computer whizkid?

But, of course, she couldn't say that.

Like Oliver, she sipped at her coffee, wrapping her hands tightly round the warm mug.

Oliver said softly, 'It's not like you to make unconsidered remarks.' He put down his mug and, stretching across the small table, folded his hands round hers. 'At a guess, I would say that the question has been niggling at you for some time. Right?'

Jessica nodded—she couldn't think of anything else to do.

'So the cool, detached Nurse Friday is interested in my personal life...'

Jessica jerked her head up. *'No!'* It was a vehement no.

His black arched eyebrows went up again. His hands tightened round hers, pressing them harder against the warm mug.

'No?' His voice was husky. 'Why not Jess? I'm interested in yours.'

He was interested in her personal life! Jessica stared into his eyes—the steel grey was softened by a misty blue. 'Your eyes are bluey grey,' she murmured, 'not grey or grey-blue.'

Oliver leaned across the narrow table until his face almost touched hers. 'That's not what it says on my passport.' His breath fanned her cheeks, his eyes held hers.

'Then your passport is…'

'Inaccurate?' he said.

Jessica nodded. 'They make you look hard, as if you've got no feelings, and yet…' She was breathless now. 'That's not true. You are a kind and caring doctor.'

'And what do you rate me as a man?'

'I don't know you well enough to venture an opinion.' Her voice wobbled.

He nodded. 'So be it.' He stood up, crossed to the sink and rinsed his mug. 'Right, let's get started.' He strode into the sitting room. 'What do you want me to do first?'

So that's it, thought Jessica, staring at him as he stood in the middle of the room surrounded by packing cases. He doesn't really care what I think of him as a man. Well, that's fine by me. I can live with that.

'Would you unpack the boxes marked ''Books'' and put them on the shelves, please? Oh, and if you can connect up the CD player, we can have some music while we're working.' Her voice was brisk.

His mouth curled into a sardonic grin. 'I think I might manage that,' he said. 'Be interesting to see if our tastes coincide.'

CHAPTER SIX

THEIR choice in music did coincide. Jessica wondered what would have happened had it been otherwise.

Would they have worked together harmoniously, emptying teachests, the music drawing them closer as the morning went on? From time to time she glanced at Oliver. She still found it astonishing that this large, aloof man, her boss, should be here in *her* cottage, unpacking *her* books as they sang along with the rich sultry voice of Ella Fitzgerald.

'You've got a lovely baritone voice,' said Jessica.

Oliver grinned and, to her delight, reddened slightly. 'Would you believe that I was a boy treble in the school choir?'

Her mind boggled. 'I find it hard to believe that you were even in the choir.' She chuckled. 'Did you wear a red frock with a frilly collar?'

'It was blue, actually.'

She laughed joyously. 'To match your almost blue eyes.'

Oliver grinned again. It made him look young and boyish. 'I don't think the powers that be had that in mind when it was designed.'

A stack of empty boxes took the place of the full ones. Hardback and paperback books began to fill the shelves on either side of the fireplace. The log fire crackled and light from the flames flickered over the colourful bindings.

'This is nice,' murmured Oliver. 'Storm raging outside, warm and cosy in here. Nothing like books to give a homely look.' He reached into the teachest in front of him and came out with a pile. 'Ah, what have we here?' He bent his head over a boxed set of half a dozen books. His face lit up. 'Oh, great. A. A. Milne's *Pooh* books. I—'

With a strangulated sound in her throat, Jessica snatched the box from him. Her face was very pale. She straightened up, holding it close to her chest.

Slowly Oliver stood up. 'What's wrong, Jess? Is there anything that I can do?' His eyes were kind, his voice like the voice he sometimes used with his patients.

'I don't want a doctor or advice.' Her voice was low and hard.

'I'm not offering as a doctor, but as a friend.'

Jessica stared at him for a long time, her eyes boring deep into his.

'Will you just *listen*?' she asked.

He nodded. 'Whenever you're ready.' Gently he squeezed her shoulders and she didn't object.

In a tight, strained voice, she plunged straight into her story. As if, if it had to be said, it was better said quickly.

'Just over eighteen months ago I lost my baby, Thomas. He was killed in a car crash caused by a drunken driver.' She crossed her arms over her abdomen and breasts, as he had seen other bereaved women do. 'I survived and wished I hadn't. The *Pooh* collection was his, a present from his godmother.'

Oliver tightened his hold on her.

'My family and close friends were marvellous, but I didn't want to live—nothing to live for.'

'Your partner?'

'Disappeared when he found that I was pregnant. I didn't mind once I got over the shock and my hurt pride.' She gave a tremulous smile. 'In fact, I was glad. Thomas was all mine, nothing to do with his father. We managed fine—he was the most darling baby, pink and soft and all mine. I wouldn't have had it any other way. I loved him like crazy.'

She drew in a deep, shuddering breath and closed her eyes. Tears squeezed out between her lids and trickled down her cheeks.

Oliver dried them with his thumbs.

'He was my whole life. I wanted to devour him. He had gentian blue eyes and smiled a lot, real smiles, he'd got past the windy stage. He was a happy, happy baby.'

'Have you a photo of him?'

'Dozens, but my favourite, taken a few days before he died, is beside my bed.'

'May I see it, Jess?' He'd have crossed his fingers had they been free. Was he pushing too much?

There was what seemed an interminable silence, and then she said, 'Yes.' She slid from beneath his hands.

He heard her go upstairs. She was gone only moments and silently handed him a silver-framed photograph when she returned.

'Even my family haven't seen this one,' she said softly. 'I kept it in my bedside drawer when I was at home, and slept with it under my pillow at night.'

To allow him to see it—what an honour! Oliver's heart beat faster.

It was an outdoor photograph taken against a fence smothered in brilliant sweet-pea blooms. Above a button nose, surprised blue eyes stared out from the tender contours of the baby face. The beginnings of a smile lifted the corners of the rosebud mouth, and silvery blond wisps of hair, touched by sunshine, ruffled in the breeze.

'He's a perfect baby,' Oliver murmured in a choked voice. 'Oh, Jess, no wonder you're sometimes so shattered when dealing with the little ones. Each one of them must be a reminder of what happened to Thomas. And yet, for most of the time, you don't let it show, though you must feel like weeping buckets.'

He smoothed her hair back and dropped a chaste kiss on her forehead.

'Why have you kept Thomas a secret? You've nothing to be ashamed of—in fact, the reverse. Rachel and the others would be most understanding, and you could talk to them when you're at a low ebb. Women are so much better at talking about these things than men.'

Jess smiled slightly. 'You don't do badly at it, and they're a great lot. But I wanted this to be a new beginning, a cut-off point from all that's happened in the last couple of years. I wanted to give the impression that I was free of any entanglements, emotional or otherwise. Do my own thing, have my own space, not get too close to anyone.'

'So what's happened in a few weeks to make you change your mind?'

Tears still shimmered in her eyes, but she managed a wobbly smile.

'You happened, and Rachel and the others, not forgetting Rory and Fred. And, of course, the patients. They make me feel useful, have given me a reason to fight back. Everyone has made me feel that I belong. I didn't want to rock the boat, go into explanations. I didn't want a load of sympathy, however genuine. It changes relationships, makes people wary of what they say.'

'Yes, I can understand that. It's a kind of emotional charity.'

'Exactly. I think it's similar to the way some of the Arundel Street patients feel and why they hate going on the social. One feels beholden and unable to make any sort of repayment. I needed tons of genuine sympathy when the accident first happened, but at some point along the way I wanted to get away from it. I'd had a near breakdown of sorts.'

'And your breakdown was your way of getting away from it.'

Abruptly, Jessica moved away from him and began pacing up and down.

'Yes. I felt as if I was being smothered with love, well meant but, you see, none of them knew about losing a baby, even my parents. I couldn't breathe, I felt I was with strangers. Physically I wasn't very fit, not well enough to do anything practical like setting up on my own again...'

'So what happened to put you on the road to recovery?'

'Dad sent me to a convalescent home run by nuns. The sister superior had been at medical school with him. It was in the wilds of Cumbria, beautiful, remote, lots of space and quiet. No one pestered me to talk or eat or anything...'

She stopped pacing. 'One day I went into the chapel and sat looking at a modern statue of the Virgin Mary and the infant Jesus. Very simple, clean lines, natural, nothing sugary about it. She was smiling slightly and gazing down at her baby...'

Jessica put her hand to her throat and closed her eyes. She was very still, like a statue herself. Her face was pale, her silvery hair touched by firelight. Oliver could see faint blue veins on her eyelids. He wanted to take her back into his arms, but didn't dare move and hardly dared breathe.

When she opened her eyes moments later she said softly, 'That was the catalyst. I wept for days. When I stopped weeping I was back more or less to normal. I was still chockfull of bitterness, but I could cope—just. You know the rest. I worked in Dad's surgery—and now I'm here, where I feel I belong.'

Oliver still felt that he shouldn't move. 'You do belong,' he murmured, 'and not just as a nurse, but in every way—to all of us, but especially to me.' He walked round the table until he was standing inches away from her. 'But you're not full of bitterness now. There's something different about you.'

She hadn't realised that he'd noticed so much.

He lifted a strand of her hair and let it slide through his fingers. 'In spite of telling me about Thomas, there's a deep well of calm within you, a calm that's not been with you until today.'

'I woke up feeling it. It just came out of nothing, and I knew that everything would be different from now on. That I could make a new start, not in the passive way that I had by moving here but on a deeper, more meaningful level.'

'Does this future include a meaningful relationship? Or is it too soon for that?'

Jessica's eyes met his. 'That depends.'

He questioned her with his eyebrows. 'On what?'

'Whether the relationship has a chance of surviving long term.' The question had surprised her. 'Why do you ask?'

He seemed surprised, too. 'I'm not sure. Wondering if perhaps, after what you went through, you would ever consider another relationship.'

Jessica shook her head. 'At this moment in time it's the last thing I want to do. Thank you for listening to me. Talking about it has rounded off the good feeling I woke up with. The utter sense of misery has gone.'

'You look better but you're still very pale. I think a little pick-me-up is called for. Stay there.' He pushed her into an armchair.

A faint smile touched her lips. 'You make me sound like a Victorian maiden with the vapours.'

'Heaven forbid. Vaporous maidens I can do without. I like my women with a streak of toughness in them.'

He disappeared into the kitchen and she heard the fridge being opened, followed by the clink of glasses and the pop of what could only be a champagne cork.

'Sorry about the tumblers,' he said moments later when he appeared, carrying two glasses. 'These are all I can find. Not really the thing for bubbly, and brandy would be better as a reviver, but I didn't bring any with me.'

'Champagne will do very nicely,' said Jessica, taking the proffered glass. 'It always tastes good even out of a tooth mug.'

'Ah, student days,' he said. 'Happy days.' He clinked his glass against hers. 'Here's to even happier days at number six Spit Cottages.'

The doorbell rang.

*   *   *

Lying in bed that night, listening to the waves lapping on the beach, subdued now that the wind had dropped, Jessica wondered what would have happened if Rachel hadn't turned up when she had. Would the vibes flowing between herself and Oliver as they'd drunk their champagne have strengthened into something more significant than friendship and goodwill?

It might have happened. And then what? 'Nothing!' she exclaimed out loud to the darkened room. 'No way! Not again, ever. Men, sex, and what does that lead to…?' She sat up and punched her pillow. She swallowed tears. She couldn't—wouldn't—open herself up to a repeat of the loss of something so precious as a baby. It just wasn't on her agenda.

She had all she wanted—this job, working with congenial people. It was challenging and filled much of her otherwise empty days. And now with this cottage, and a garden that would also be a challenge, she would be able to fill her off duty time, too.

Rachel's arrival had been a blessing, and the day had been fun. The wine and pizza she had brought, together with Oliver's pink champagne—'Not vintage,' he'd apologised, 'but nice and bubbly, party stuff,'—and the smoked-salmon sandwiches had made sure of that.

They had all worked hard until after five when Oliver had announced—reluctantly, Jessica had thought—that he'd have to be off. He'd had a visit to make to the hospital. So it had been an Arundel Street patient—the private patients went to the Nightingale.

'Anyone I know?' Jessica asked.

'Yes, Naomi Walker, the little Jamaican girl, suspected brittle bones. Rory rang last night. Apparently she had a bad fall yesterday and she's fractured her femur. A nasty comminuted fracture. It's going to take time to put together.'

'Oh, poor little girl, give her my love. And poor Mrs Walker, as if she hasn't enough on her plate.'

'Gloria will cope, she always does.'

'Yes, but it's not fair.'

'Life isn't fair—hadn't you noticed?' said Oliver, and the laughter that had been in his eyes most of the day, had suddenly vanished.

'Hey, come on you two, you're getting a bit heavy, aren't you?' said Rachel.

They both apologised simultaneously, and Oliver offered Rachel a lift.

'Well...' she said uncertainly, looking at Jessica. 'There's still a fair bit to do, and Jessica will be on her own in this...' She shuddered and waved her hand toward the darkening window.

Jessica laughed and assured her that she would be all right on her own.

'Well, if you're sure.'

'Positive. And I can't thank you both enough for your help and the goodies. It's made the day I moved into number six Spit Cottages a day to remember.'

It had been memorable for the sharing of her secret with Oliver. His tender compassion and understanding had been like balm to her emotional wounds. Memorable, too, for the discovery of this new Oliver Pendragon, yet another dimension to the enigmatic man who was her boss.

The wind and rain had stopped by the time he and Rachel left, but the sky was dark with low black clouds. She stood in the doorway and watched the taillights of his car disappear up the lane.

Had Oliver, she wondered, regretted Rachel's arrival? He had shown no sign of it.

Except perhaps for that knowing gleam in his eye as he'd said goodnight.

Sunday dawned, a mellow autumn day. The sun beamed gently on the almost still waters of the estuary. Jessica flung all the windows wide and breathed in the salty air. She had slept deeply and dreamlessly for the first time in a long while. And she felt less empty, less bereft than she had at any time since the accident.

A healing sleep, her mother would have called it.

The phone rang. 'Hello, darling,' said her mother as soon as she lifted the receiver. 'How did it go yesterday? The weather was awful for you. We were so sorry that we couldn't be there to help.'

It was lovely to hear her mother's voice. 'Mum. How did you know that I was thinking about you?'

'Because I was thinking about you, too, love.' She gave her rich chuckle. 'But, there, I'm besotted where my children are concerned, and none of you are ever long out of my thoughts. Anyway, enough of this. How are you managing?'

'Fine. Rachel came over to help. She's our receptionist, I've told you about her. She's a gem under her sophisticated veneer. We kept going on the pizza and wine that she brought, and got everything more or less straight. Today I'll potter around, sorting my CDs and books and hanging a few prints.'

'You should try to get out in the sunshine for a bit. Winter will soon be upon us.'

'I'm going beachcombing along the shore presently. There should be lots of flotsam and jetsam thrown up by yesterday's storm.'

'Good. Phone if you need anything darling. We can be with you in three hours or so. Bye, love.'

'Bye.'

They're afraid I might crack up again, Jessica thought as she slowly put the phone down—and why didn't I tell Mum about Oliver?

Even the slightest niggle of disappointment because Oliver hadn't rung, though there was no reason why he should have, didn't prevent Jessica from sleeping well again on Sunday night.

Spending much of the day on the beach in the fresh air and sunshine, it worked wonders. She collected a treasure trove of odd-shaped pieces of wood and beautiful shells and pebbles, which she piled in the back porch to be sorted later. How *had* Oliver known about the porch in a small terraced cottage?

Starting off for work on Monday morning, was a mild adventure. Her usually reliable Mini, though housed in the timber garage at the side of the house, refused to start.

An old man with a stick hobbled down the path of number five. He bent to look through the window. 'Want any help, love?' he asked.

A push might do the trick, thought Jessica, then wryly decided that it would be followed smartly by a myocardial infarction.

She beamed the elderly gentleman a smile. 'Thanks for the offer, Mr...?'

'Jackson.'

'Mr Jackson, but I've just got to wait or I'll flood the engine.' She stuck her hand out of the window. 'I'd better introduce myself. I'm Jessica Friday, I've just moved in next door.'

Old eyes twinkled at her as a bony, arthritic hand clasped hers. 'Yes, so I noticed. Could have chosen a better day for it, but at least it made the removal blokes get a move on. Never seen 'em move so fast.'

Jessica laughed. Twitching curtains. Small town ethos of keeping an eye on your neighbour. Not that Porthampton was a small town, it was a busy city, but the Spit was small, almost remote. It was just like being in her home village, where all comings and goings were noted. 'That's true, and they did a good job.' She sneaked a look at her watch.

Mr Jackson nodded. 'Yep, she'll start now,' he said. 'She just don't like the salt wind. If I was you, I'd put a blanket over her at night, even though she's in the garage.'

'I'll do that,' Jessica promised. She turned the key in the ignition. The engine purred into life.

'A bit of patience, that's all that's needed,' muttered Mr Jackson, as she moved off up the lane.

Jessica gave him a wave, and he waved back.

The Arundel Street surgery was almost full when she arrived. Both Jane and Dorothy were hard at it, processing the queue at the reception desk.

'You've cut it fine,' said Jane in an aside, as Jessica eased her way round the desk. 'You've got a bunch of patients already.' She grinned. 'Some of them with kids in tow.'

Jessica groaned as she took the list from Jane. 'Kids and cervical smears just don't go together,' she said dryly. 'You either have to take them into the cubicle with Mum, or hope they'll stay penned in with the toys for a few minutes.'

'Sophie used to say that she could do with another pair of hands, and the smears list has grown since then. If Dot or I could help we would, but you can see how it is.' Jane waved her hand at the queue.

'Perhaps,' Dot, who'd obviously been listening with half an ear, interjected, 'my Kelly might come and help out during the holidays. You know, look after the kids—that's if the boss wouldn't mind.'

'Mind what?' asked Oliver, suddenly appearing in the wide doorway leading to the passage and the consulting rooms.

Jessica's heart jolted at the sight of him. She took a jerky breath. 'Oh, it's a bit complicated.

Perhaps we should explain later. I must get on and Jane and Dot are busy.'

Oliver smiled and raised an eyebrow. 'So what's new?' he said. 'Come on, no secrets, ladies. Is this something that calls for a staff get-together?' He looked at their three flushed faces.

'Might be a good idea,' said Dot. 'Haven't had one for ages.'

'True, then the sooner the better. How are you all placed for after work tonight? We could meet down at the Festival Arms and combine business with pleasure. Shall we say eight-thirty? Then Rory will be able to make it after surgery.'

'Suits me,' said Dot. 'Give me time to feed my brood.'

Jane nodded. 'And me,' she confirmed.

Oliver looked at Jessica. 'Jessica? I know you've only just moved in, but can you spare a couple of hours? We'll be finished at Berkley House by six.'

Why did she feel that he was willing her to join them? She felt the colour mounting her cheeks. Be casual.

'Yes, of course, no problem.'

'Good! OK, so that's settled. We can do with a night out. Now let's all get cracking and earn our keep.'

With a smile for the three of them, he went off to his consulting room.

Jessica collected her list of patients and made for her treatment room. Her heart, which for so long had lain like a painful, unmoving lump in her chest, seemed to expand and flutter.

She crossed her hands flat, over her breast. *But I'll never forget you my darling, never.*

She took a long, deep, shuddering breath and returned to the waiting room to call in her first patient.

Meg Jenkins, a thirty-five-year-old primigravida, had given birth to her baby six months earlier and was in for her first smear since the baby's birth.

A big, blonde, smiling woman, she bounced vigorously into the treatment room and plonked the baby car seat down on the floor. 'Heather,' she said, her voice proud.

The baby made a chirruping sound and dimpled a smile at Jessica, who pursed her lips and made a kissing sound back. She wanted to stroke the soft downy cheek, but refrained and concentrated on what Meg was saying.

'Well, Nurse, Dr Pendragon said I should come when my periods returned to normal, and I reckon that they're about as normal as they'll ever be. I never have been what you might call regular.'

'Then I shouldn't worry about it—that is your normal. Are you still breast-feeding Heather?'

Meg climbed onto the couch and got herself into position for her smear. 'As much as I can, but I seem to be drying up, which is a pity. Nature's way is the cheapest, and it's magic to cuddle her and feel her sucking away.'

Jessica bent her head and peered under the sheet draped over Meg's knees. 'Just inserting the speculum to keep your vagina open,' she said, steadying her hand. 'And now the spatula. It won't hurt. I'm going to scrape a few cells from the cervix to be sent to the lab.' She came out from under the sheet. 'There, all finished. You can tidy up now.'

'No one's ever explained it to me like that before,' said Meg. 'And I've often wanted to know exactly what you do and how you get to the cells. Do you explain it to everyone?'

'Yes, ever since I had my own first smear, I do it as a matter of course,' said Jessica. 'I knew what to expect but I still felt sort of vulnerable. It occurred to me that most women must feel the same or worse because they don't know what's happening.'

'You know what, Nurse? You're brilliant.' Meg picked up the baby seat and blew a raspberry at baby Heather.

Jessica kept her head bent over the glass slides. 'We aim to please,' she said lightly.

There were a several more smears to do, but no more beautiful, tiny babies like Heather to turn her to jelly. Several toddlers needed to be distracted with varying degrees of success. One very difficult five-year-old boy kept bobbing in and out of the cubicle and stretched her patience to the limit. This, of course, made his mother tense. It took all Jessica's skill to obtain a satisfactory specimen.

Her last patient, Brenda Hawthorne, fifty-four, was in the throes of the menopause and very uptight. She had recently started a course of HRT, but it hadn't had time to be effective and she was thinking of giving up on it.

'It will begin to kick in quite soon,' assured Jessica, 'and you'll feel much better. Many women describe it as giving them a new lease of life, so stick with it.'

Brenda looked sceptical. You're not kidding me, are you, Nurse?'

'Promise you I'm not. If it doesn't begin to work in a couple of weeks' time, you can come back and sort me out.'

Brenda actually smiled. 'You can count on it,' she said, as she left the treatment room.

Jessica stretched and heaved a sigh of relief. The morning was over. She had skipped coffee, but decided that she would snatch a cup, before going back to the cottage for a sandwich. Living between the two surgeries was already paying dividends. This afternoon she would be working at Berkley House.

Working with Oliver, talking with Oliver. Would he mention Saturday? Her heart did a sort of double beat, and her hand shook a little as she poured boiling water onto the coffee granules.

'Here, let me. You look positively dangerous. Boiling water's a lethal weapon.'

Oliver took the kettle from her and finished pouring.

Jessica felt the colour flow in and out of her face. She said crossly, 'How did you manage to creep up on me like that?'

He pointed to his shoes. They were chunky brown brogues. 'Rubber soles,' he said.

Funny, she hadn't noticed them before. Yet they went with the rest of his casual Arundel Street image, cord trousers and sweaters. He always wore highly polished black lace-ups at Berkley Square.

Jessica took the mug of coffee he handed her with a now-steady hand.

He poured one for himself and took a sip. 'A spot of caffeine does wonders after a busy session, doesn't it?' His eyes searched her face. Wonderful, her eyes had lost their dark sombre expression, the gold flecks were there. Had he been responsible for that, just because he had listened?

'You look better, if a bit whacked,' he said.

She snorted indignantly. 'There was this beastly, spoilt little five-year-old, who would keep bobbing in and out of the cubicle when I was trying to do his mum's smear. A grim reminder that kids are not always angels.'

His lip was curled up at one corner in what she supposed was a sceptical grin. 'Oh, come on, Jess, whenever were you, a tough nurse from an East End hospital, fazed by a naughty boy, large or small? We've only worked together for a few weeks, but I know you well enough to know that. In fact, I know you very well indeed, Jess.'

Jess! Twice in one short speech. And how well did he know her apart from what she had told him about Thomas? Not that there was anything else to know. Rather it was he who remained a mystery. Stern, steely-eyed and austere at times, keeping everyone at a distance. Soft and gentle at others. An enigmatic man. A secretive man. She wanted to know more about him.

She closed her eyes. No way did she want him to read her thoughts.

He chuckled and blew on her eyelids, his lips very close. 'You can't avoid looking at me for ever, Jess.'

When she opened her eyes a moment later, he had gone as stealthily as he had arrived.

CHAPTER SEVEN

IT WAS a blessing that they were busy at the consulting rooms that afternoon. It stopped Jessica dwelling on Oliver's last words and squashed the memory of his breath on her eyelids. The patients at Berkley House were always well spaced out, giving Oliver time between consultations to make phone calls and do paperwork.

This afternoon, though, he'd agreed to see an extra patient at the request of a local GP. He informed Jessica in the middle of the session when she was laying up an examination trolley for the next patient. His voice was brisk, businesslike, as if the incident at Arundel Street had never taken place.

Jessica matched his professional tone. 'When are you fitting her in?'

'After I've seen Frank Lowe. He shouldn't take too long. You've got everything ready for me to do a PR.'

It was a statement, not a question. He knew she would have anticipated that he'd want to do a post-operative rectal on Mr Lowe, who'd had an haemorrhoidectomy.

She nodded.

'Apparently,' he continued, speaking from the communicating door between the treatment room and his consulting room, 'this patient, Ms Catlyn Lafont—and she's adamant about the *Ms*—refuses to open up to Marie Watts, her regular GP. Though I can't imagine why. Marie's an excellent doctor. For some reason, this Lafont woman asked for me personally.'

Jessica made herself turn round to face him. Avoid eye contact, she reminded herself, and focused on his mouth. Not a brilliant idea—it was a reminder of the way he had blown on her eyelids. Ridiculous.

She cleared her throat. 'Sounds like another mystery patient, another Mr Roger Jefferson.' Good, that came out rather well. 'By the way, have you heard anything about him? Do you know how he's doing?' One of the things she most enjoyed about general practice was following a patient's progress.

'He's had surgery. They think they've removed all the tumour, but can't be sure. It was pretty massive because he'd left it so long. He's going to need a lot of follow-up treatment and a lengthy recovery period. The outcome isn't all that certain. There may be brain damage.'

Jessica forgot about no eye contact at the same moment as Oliver crossed from the doorway to stand in front of her.

She suddenly wanted—needed—to make contact. She touched his dark suited arm. 'Oh, the poor man, all that high-pressure business. A fat lot of good it's done him.' To her chagrin, a tear trickled down her cheek.

It seemed natural when Oliver brushed it away with a forefinger. He lifted her hand from his sleeve and brought it to his lips. 'You're almost too soft-hearted for this business,' he murmured.

'I've been doing it a long time. Nursing's my life.' She glimmered a smile through her tears. 'I'm an East End nursing toughie, remember?'

'I suppose it was a baby that made you as soft as butter this morning?'

The steel-grey eyes, which weren't always steel, didn't miss a thing. They were *his* cover, she suddenly realised, just as hers had been a cool detachment until he'd breached it. And she knew in that moment without a doubt that behind the grey eyes he, too, concealed a secret. Well, secrets could fester, leave a bitterness that lingered. He had persuaded her to come clean and cry on his shoulder, and already she felt a new woman.

There would be blips, just as there had been this morning over baby Heather, but the future, which had held nothing, now held hope. She must persuade him to talk.

She said quietly, 'I've told you my secret. Why don't you tell me yours?'

The wry thought occurred that it was like making a childhood pact.

'I haven't—' he started to say.

Jessica pressed a finger to his lips. 'Perhaps we all have secrets, some lesser or greater than others. Perhaps they are important, perhaps some should be shared.'

Oliver raised his eyebrows. 'Wise words,' he said. 'Now go and repair your make-up and greet my next patient as your usual immaculate self.'

What sort of answer is that? Jessica fumed as she pressed shine control moisturiser onto her nose and cheeks. And where does it leave me?

* * *

Frank Lowe came and went in under half an hour, delighted that the operation on his haemmorrhoids had been successful. 'I owe you,' he said, shaking Oliver's hand, 'for getting everything sorted out so quickly.' He turned to Jessica. 'And you, too, Nurse, for being so helpful and discreet.'

Both Oliver and Jessica murmured that it was their job. 'But you do it so well,' said Mr Lowe. He drew out a cheque-book. 'Have either of you got a favourite charity?'

'Cot deaths,' said Oliver and Jessica in unison. They looked at each other in surprise as Mr Lowe wrote out a cheque.

Jessica gloated over the five-hundred-pound cheque when the man had left. 'That was generous of him,' she said, aware that it probably represented about five pence to him. He was something in shipping, one of the new wealthy admin and executive types who had sprung up in and round Porthampton. A few years ago he wouldn't have dreamed of having private treatment, but now took it in his stride.

'Nice gesture,' agreed Oliver. 'Why cot deaths, Jess?'

'Because I saw three in A and E. Believe me, a mother frantically trying to revive her already dead baby is something you just don't forget. Why is it your favourite charity, Oliver?'

The internal phone on his desk buzzed. He snatched up the receiver. 'Yes?' he said.

'Ms Lafont is here,' Rachel announced.

'Show her in, please, Rachel.'

'I'll disappear.' Jessica moved toward the door.

'No. She's a new, youngish female. I'd like her to know that there's someone else around. You can go after I've introduced you.'

'All right.' She moved to the curtained examination couch in the corner and began retidying it.

There was a tap on the door.

'Ms Lafont,' announced Rachel, and disappeared, closing the door behind her.

A small woman in a tailored black trouser suit walked briskly across the room, her hand outstretched, straight towards Oliver. Her hair was black and cropped short.

She's not much bigger than Lucinda, thought Jessica, and as striking in her own way. But why so severe?

Oliver met her halfway, his polished, courteous manner much in evidence. 'Good afternoon, Ms Lafont.' He engulfed her small hand in his, and with his other hand motioned to Jessica. 'Jessica Friday,' he said. 'My confidential nurse.'

Ms Lafont inclined her head toward Jessica. 'And chaperone?' she queried dryly. There was a smile in her voice.

Oliver grinned. 'Ah, you've caught me out. Nurse won't be staying…'

'You just wanted to let me know she was around.'

'Caught again.'

'Actually…' Ms Lafont slanted a smile at Jessica '…I wouldn't in the least mind Nurse Friday sitting in on my consultation. As a woman around my own age, she might offer a useful opinion. I want advice on a moral as well as a medical issue.'

'Two questions.' said Oliver. 'Why not stick with Dr Watts? And why me?'

'Dr Watts is on the point of retiring. She may not be sympathetic to my problem and, if she is, may not be around to see me through the next few years—or however long it takes to achieve my goal.'

'Right, but why me? What makes you think that I shall be any more sympathetic to your problem than Dr Watts?'

'You're the right age, you're a qualified obstetrician and gynaecologist with an excellent reputation. As a freelance journalist I attended one of your lectures at the university hospital, and liked what I heard. I believe we are on the same wave length.'

Oliver eyed her thoughtfully over the desk. Ms Lafont eyed him back.

'So you have an obstetric or gynaecological problem.'

'I don't know yet—that's what I want you to find out before I decide whether or not to go ahead and get pregnant.'

'Does your partner—?'

'I haven't got a partner, I don't want one. But I do want a baby, provided I'm fit and able to bear one to term.'

'Ideally, it takes two,' said Oliver mildly, 'to produce a baby.'

'Ideally,' replied Ms Lafont, 'but there are other ways, are there not? Anonymous donated sperm, for instance.'

Oliver leaned back in his chair and knuckled his hands under his chin. 'If we're talking *in vitro* fertilisation in a perfectly healthy uterus, with all the rest of your equipment for natural conception in order, Ms Lafont, I'm afraid I can't help.' His voice was cool. He lowered his hands to the arms of his chair and levered himself up.

Catlyn Lafont tilted her head to look at him. Her strong yet refined features were strained. '*Please*, Dr Pendragon, let me explain why before you make a decision. Surely emotional as well as physical reasons can be taken into consideration.'

Say yes, Oliver, Jessica silently pleaded. This woman may look cool and together but she needs help.

As if he'd got her message, Oliver sank slowly back onto his chair. He pushed his cuff back and glanced at his watch.

'All right Miss Lafont, I can give you a quarter of an hour to plead your cause.'

Catlyn Lafont's story came out in short, disjointed, staccato sentences. It must have hurt her to the point of agony to tell it.

'My partner was killed in Afghanistan seven years ago. He was a freelance photographer. I only learned later that it was on the same day that I had a miscarriage. I was five months pregnant. I was in Africa, covering a story about tribal warfare. It was to be my last overseas assignment till after the baby…'

Her dark eyes sparkled with held-back tears. She fished in her bag for a handkerchief. 'There was a raid on the village I was in by a neighbouring tribe…' She shuddered. 'They killed, raped…' Oliver got up and walked round the desk. He poured water from his carafe and handed her the glass. 'Were you raped, Miss Lafont?' he asked, his voice gentle but matter-of-fact.

Her face went porcelain white, her voice was barely audible. 'I was on the point of being…' She gulped down some water. Her hand shook. 'The man was crouching over me… He was attacked by another man. I passed out. Loss of blood, apparently. When I came round I was in the local mission hospital and I'd lost the baby.'

I'd lost the baby! The words hung in the air. They were all silent for a few moments.

Jessica found herself tucking her hands under her arms and hugging her breasts. Her lower abdomen ached. Any miscarriage was agonising, but this…

For an instant Oliver laid his hand on Ms Lafont's shoulder, then he moved slowly back round his desk. His face was impassive, but his eyes were steel-grey. Jessica guessed that he was seething, and searching for the right words.

When he spoke, his voice had changed to a gravelly gentleness. 'I owe you an apology, Ms Lafont, and I'm grateful to you for making me listen. You're absolutely right, your emotional condition is as valid as your physical condition for wanting a baby by an anonymous donor.'

He leaned his elbows on the table and rested his chin on clasped hands so that his eyes were on a level with hers.

'I have to warn you, though, that many responsible physicians in the fertility field will be reluctant about inducing a pregnancy in a single woman. Even women with loving partners find the process traumatic. We'll have to do a bit of searching around to find the right expert.'

'Does the *we* mean that you'll take me on as a patient?' Some colour had returned to her face, and it shone with sudden hope.

Oliver's voice was back to normal. 'I will take you on as a patient if you wish it, but…' he held up his hand '…that doesn't mean that I shall happily agree to artificial insemination. For one thing, I'm not an expert in that field. You would be in someone else's hands for that procedure.'

'But *if* treatment was agreed, would you see me through, deliver my baby?'

He took his time answering. 'I don't do much hands-on obstetric work these days, too busy, but when I do I have a first-class team who work with me at the Nightingale. That's a private nursing home with top-of-the-range facilities—but it costs, just as AID will cost.'

Catlyn waved the costs away. 'I made up my mind that I would have another baby when I could afford it, just for Stewart.' Her knuckles showed white as her fingers clutched her bag. 'I've worked like a Trojan, establishing my reputation, now I virtually command my own fees. But I won't have another man involved—I couldn't…' She took a deep, shuddering breath. 'This must be Stewart's baby.'

Jessica moved to stand beside her and closed her hand over Catlyn's white knuckles, offering female solidarity. There was nothing else she could do to help—only Oliver could do that. But would he? In spite of the reasons Catlyn Lafont wanted a baby, in spite of her natural abhorrence of sexual intercourse after what had happened, she was a single woman.

Would she be accepted as a suitable subject for AID intervention?

Oliver spoke at last, his voice soft, firm. 'But it won't be Stewart's baby, my dear, will it? That is one of the things you'll have to come to terms with. It would be your baby, *not* Stewart's. An anonymous donor may be possible, though the practice of any intervention is ringed round with all sorts of safeguards to protect the mother and the baby. As I said, we would have to get expert opinion on this.'

The internal phone buzzed. 'Yes, Rachel?' Rachel's voice came over clearly, announcing the next patient. 'Ask him to wait just a few more minutes, please.'

Catlyn's hands were suddenly gripping Jessica's. She leaned forward as Oliver put down the phone, and her bag slipped from her lap. 'But you will do it, won't you—deliver my baby?'

Oliver nodded and his lips curved into a smile. 'You've won me round, Ms Lafont.

Arranging matters will take time. There are no short cuts. I can't promise success but I'll do my damnedest to help you.'

Catlyn closed her eyes for a moment and breathed in deeply. When she opened them, she was smiling. 'Thank you, Dr Pendragon. The fact that you're prepared to help makes me very happy. And, please, will you call me Cat? And you, too, Nurse. All my friends do. I hope we might be seeing quite a lot of each other in the future. Ms Lafont's a clumsy title and I don't much like it—it's simply a shield.'

Another shield, thought Jessica.

Cat Lafont had already regained her cool.

Oliver's expressive eyebrows shot up. 'Of course, that's your byline pseudonym, isn't it? C. A. T. Frobisher, the Kate Adie of the newspapers. I didn't recognise you from these postage-stamp pictures they put at the top of your piece each Sunday. Not very flattering, but I like your work—good stuff.'

Cat—it suited her, she was like a small, sleek black cat—stood up, too. 'Thank you. Yes, C. A. T. Frobisher is my byline. Frobisher is my mother's maiden name—she was persistent, too.' She dimpled a smile at Oliver as she shook hands across the desk. 'So what's the next move, Doctor? I want to get started as soon as possible. At thirty-four I feel time is against me.'

Oliver held her hand a fraction longer than necessary, Jessica thought. Because she's another Lucinda, dainty, pretty and clever? A tremor of self-disgust shook her. Catlyn bore no similarity to selfish Lucinda. This was a woman who had suffered, a woman she could relate to.

'On your way out, make an appointment with Rachel to see me again as soon as possible. Tell her that I'll need at least an hour. Come prepared to give me a full medical history—childhood and recent illnesses, operations, and so on. I shall give you a complete physical, and do blood and other tests—make sure you're basically fit. And if we do find someone to accept you for AID, you'll have to go through the procedure all over again. It's going to be a long and tedious haul.'

'I can tough it out for as long as it takes. It'll be worth it in the end.'

The last patient was a well-known actor appearing at the Playhouse Theatre in Porthampton. He had an ear infection for which Oliver prescribed an antibiotic. He left just after six.

'So, what did you think of our Ms Lafont?' asked Oliver, appearing in the doorway after the actor had left.

Jessica continued clearing up in the treatment room. 'In what way?' she asked cautiously.

He shrugged. 'Any way at all—as a nurse with a patient, as one woman assessing another.'

Jessica paused in wiping down the dressings trolley. 'I think she's a brave woman—must be to go to all those dangerous places in search of a story. I think she still hasn't got over the horrific thing that happened to her—what woman would? She's determined, but she's hiding behind a brittle mask, pretending to be very together.'

'But not together enough to handle single parenthood?'

'I didn't say that. Having a baby, it might be what she needs.'

'But what about the baby's needs? Would it be right for he or she to substitute for a dead lover or another dead baby?

Jessica said in a tight voice, 'Look, Oliver—' the 'Oliver' had slipped out, she meant to be formal at work '—I really don't know. I'm not qualified to comment, but there are plenty of people around who are. In fact, she'll have to have counselling before treatment, won't she, to determine if the baby option is the right thing?'

She crouched down to clear and wipe the bottom shelf. 'She may not be considered suitable for AID. I doubt she'll stand a chance of being treated. As a single physically healthy woman she won't exactly be welcomed with open arms.'

'You seem to be pretty well informed about the procedure.'

'There was an article in a recent nursing mag.' She carefully fed dirty needles into the sharps container. Her heart bumped uncomfortably against her ribs.

'I thought perhaps you'd had a more direct interest in AID.'

'No.' She began wiping down the glass and chrome trolley.

'You've already done that.' Oliver's voice was quiet, sympathetic.

'One can't be too thorough.'

He crossed the room, took the cloth out of her hand and dropped it into the basin of antiseptic, then turned Jessica to face him.

'Did you consider AID after Thomas died? You seem to have an affinity with our Ms Lafont.'

Jessica produced a wry smile. 'Full marks for perceptiveness, Dr Pendragon. Not many men would appreciate the subtleties of the connection.' She touched his arm. 'Thank you for being prepared to help her.'

He barked a short laugh. 'I could feel you ordering me to do so. What chance had a mere man got, faced with two strong-minded women?' He frowned. 'Did you seriously consider artificial insemination?'

'Briefly, but I wouldn't have got far. I didn't have the strong emotional reason that Cat has.' She looked at him steadily. 'Sure, I'd lost a baby, but that happens to thousands of women every year. I never thought I'd say this, but I think I'll get over it—remember all the joy Thomas brought me as well as the devastation of losing him. One day I might even have a chance to have another baby—without help, Catlyn can't.'

'You're very brave.'

She shook her head. 'No. Thanks to using you as a shoulder to cry on, I've got things into some sort of perspective.' She looked at the white wall clock above the glassed-in shelves of clinical equipment. 'I must dash if I'm to get home and make myself presentable for our meeting at the Festival Arms. Musn't let the side down.'

Oliver took hold of her hands. 'You don't have to come, you're whacked out.'

'No, I'm not, and I want to come. Arundel Street's important to me.'

'I'll collect you in a taxi.'

'No, thank you, I'll go in my own car. I want to be free to leave when I want to.' She smiled to take the sting out of her words. The last thing she wanted right now was to be in a confined space with Oliver. She felt churned up, unsure of herself.

His eyes were kind, understanding, which somehow made it worse. 'That means that neither of us can drink,' he said ruefully. 'Jane and Dorothy will be disappointed. They enjoy their gin and tonics, and I like to make these meetings social occasions. We get so little time to chat at work. I usually down a few pints with them.'

'You're blackmailing me.'

'In a good cause. Like so many working women, they don't get many outings. They'll feel awkward drinking if we're not. You can choose when to order the taxi back—promise.'

Rat-a-tat-tat. It was just after eight.

'Love the fishy knocker,' said Oliver, when Jessica opened the door. 'Didn't notice it on Saturday, what with the weather and the removal men.'

'Yes, it is rather attractive, isn't it? Bold and brassy and fitting for what was once a fisherman's cottage.' Jessica slid out of the door and closed it behind her. 'You don't think it's a bit twee, do you?' She smiled brightly up at him.

For once he was caught off guard and looked fleetingly surprised. Because she hadn't asked him in, or because he hadn't expected to find her so cheerful? Or perhaps her clothes had surprised him. His eyes had widened when he'd first seen her, skimming over her from top to bottom when she'd opened the door. It didn't matter—it was all part of her strategy.

She'd put on her brightest clothes in keeping with her new status. A raspberry red, silk, polo-necked, sleeveless sweater contrasted dramatically with her silver-blonde hair, and was topped by a jazzy, multicoloured woollen jacket slung round her shoulders, with hip-hugging cream linen trousers and chunky trainers rounding off the smart but casual image.

He recovered his cool quickly. 'Not a bit twee,' he said, following her down the path. 'It might have even been there from when the cottages were built. I read somewhere that fishermen set great store by omens. Maybe your fish was a good omen.'

Jessica settled herself in the taxi. She laughed. 'Maybe it was all part of the tarting-up process by the previous owners when they put in central heating and new plumbing and wiring.'

Oliver laughed, too. 'I like my explanation best,' he said. 'More romantic.'

Dorothy and Jane were just sitting down when Jessica and Oliver arrived at the pub.

'My round, ladies,' said Oliver.

Most rounds seemed to be his, Jessica noted as the evening wore on. He ignored her attempt, and Dot's and Jane's, to buy a round. Only when Rory arrived, did he allow him get one round of drinks in.

'Your chauvinism is showing,' Jessica murmured under cover of the general conversation.

A smile quirked the corner of his mouth. 'Does it bother you?'

'I don't think so, it's just unusual these days.'

'Then you've been going out with the wrong men—or impecunious medical students.'

For wrong men read man, she thought wryly.

'Something like that,' she said lightly, 'but, then, there are a lot of them about in the closed world of medicine.'

'Wrong men or students?'

'Both.'

Dorothy rapped on the table. 'I vote,' she said, 'now that Rory's arrived, that we call this meeting to order before we're all too tiddly to think straight.' She waved her glass in the air—it was her second gin and tonic.

Rory pulled a face. 'No chance of me getting smashed on a shandy. I'm on call.'

'You're right, Dot, time we got down to business, so fire away. What are these changes you want to make at the surgery?' Oliver gave her a wide encouraging smile.

'Well, first of all, if someone could look after the kids when Jessica's trying to do the cervical smears... You explain, Jessica.'

'Dot's right. It can be a problem when there are a lot of kids, like today. It slows things down and some of the mums can't relax, which doesn't help matters.' She was glad that she'd told him that morning about the irritating small boy who'd been such a nuisance.

Oliver's eyebrows rose. 'So what are you suggesting, a sort of crèche?'

Jessica grinned. 'Nothing so grand, but someone to keep an eye on the kids in the play area in the waiting room would help. Perhaps it could be extended a little. I'm sure the mums would be happy to leave them if there was someone to supervise. It could work for you and Rory, too, when you wanted to examine a patient and there was a child in tow.'

'And had you got someone in mind for this task who wouldn't cost the earth to employ?' He looked from Jessica, to Dot, to Jane, his eyes teasing. All three blushed.

'You heard,' accused Jessica, 'this morning. You were listening before you appeared. Don't they say that listeners never hear any good of themselves?'

He ignored the jibe. 'Acute hearing is one of my attributes,' he said, and his eyes added, for her alone, as well as being perceptive. Only perhaps that was in her imagination.

'So what do you think of the idea?'

'Basically sensible, but what about in term time when Kelly's at school?' He grinned at Dot and Jane. 'I don't suppose either of you have a nice nanny figure tucked away somewhere who would be glad of a top-up on her pension?'

'My mum,' said Jane promptly. 'She was a care assistant at the hospital, but she's just been retired. I bet she'd enjoy coming for the company, and she's a wizard with kids.'

Oliver beamed. 'She sounds perfect,' he said. 'I'd like to meet her. You know when I'll be in, Jane. Fix something for before or after surgery, as soon as possible. Now, any other business?'

They thrashed out the perennial problem of how the waiting lists might be reduced or spread better.

'The thing is…' said Dot. Her several drinks seemed to have sharpened her wits, not dulled them. 'Half the patients in the waiting room are emergencies who should go to Casualty, but they come to us instead. They feel safer with us and they don't have to get a bus as they would to the hospital. Bus fares cost money.'

'So what it comes down to,' said Oliver, after the argument had swung back and forth for ten minutes, 'is the need for another pair of hands, either medical or nursing. What do you think, Jessica, Rory?'

Rory grinned. 'Great, if we can find someone who'd fit in and be prepared to work twenty-four hours a day for a slave-driver of a boss.'

Oliver punched him lightly on the shoulder. 'You wait, my lad, till you're the only medic for miles around, then you'll know what hard work's about.' He turned to Jessica. 'What about you, Jessica, do you think it would be a good idea to bring someone else in?'

He was sitting close to her and she couldn't avoid meeting his eyes. They were serious, his voice was serious, he *wanted* her opinion. It was as if hers was the only opinion he wanted. She had the curious sensation that for a moment they were alone in the noisy, crowded pub.

This shouldn't be happening. This was what she had geared herself up to avoid. This was why she hadn't invited him into the cottage. To be close to him spelt danger, intimacy. She had changed in a few weeks but she wasn't ready for that—yet.

She blinked to break the tension between them, and took a sip of her drink. 'I rather agree with Rory about it having to be the right person. Whoever it is must fit in. Arundel Street works because every one gels.' She coloured slightly, and added apologetically, 'Though I'm only a newcomer. Perhaps I shouldn't be saying this.'

Rory, Dot and Jane made noises of disagreement.

'You fitted in from the start,' said Dot. 'You're one of us.'

Jessica felt a warm glow steal over her. Like Rachel, they were new friends, but true friends.

Oliver smiled at everyone. 'Right, I'll mull it over for a day or two, see if I can come up with anything. Meanwhile, if anyone has any bright ideas, let's have them.'

The other ever-present problem was how to find more storage space for records. The spare room in Fred's flat was full to bursting.

'Don't know why we have to keep them,' grumbled Dot. 'We've got everything on computer.'

'Well, the powers that be insist on it,' said Oliver, 'and I must say it's convenient to take notes with one when visiting a patient. Don't you agree, Rory?'

'Oh, yeah, sure,' Rory mumbled vaguely, tearing his eyes away from a spectacular blonde leaning against the bar.

Oliver caught his eye. 'Nice,' he murmured. 'Now, what about another drink?'

'It'll be my fourth.' Dot giggled. 'But if you're offering, Doc, what the hell. I only do this once in a blue moon.'

'Then I think your liver will survive,' said Oliver, and shouldered his way to the bar to fetch more drinks.

CHAPTER EIGHT

OLIVER'S got no right to have such charm. No, not charm—insipid word—charisma, thought Jessica, lying in bed and willing sleep to come.

He'd appeared distant and aloof when she'd first met him, but it had taken only a few weeks to give the lie to that. Oh, he could be reserved, play the distinguished physician, but the more one learned about him, the more it was obvious that beneath the sophisticated exterior was a man of warmth with a soft heart.

Today had been a case in point. His treatment of Catlyn Lafont proved that. And his perceptiveness about herself. He'd sensed that something was wrong when most men would never have noticed, or would have shied away from it, whereas he...

Her thoughts circled back to the cervical smear session and baby Heather. There had been an instant of sharp pain as she'd compared the peach-soft face with Thomas's, but it hadn't lingered. She'd been able to get on with her work with a calm that wouldn't have been possible before her confession to Oliver. That had been the breakthrough.

He was a man of many parts. Casually friendly with everyone, without being patronising. She smiled, remembering how he'd made a couple of pints last the evening, while appearing to match Dot's consumption of gin and tonics. There'd been laughter in his blue-grey eyes and his lovely, beautiful mouth... She yawned, turned on her side, hugged her pillow and fell asleep.

She woke to the sound of gulls screaming overhead and leapt out of bed. *She wanted to get on with the day, get to work. She wanted to see Oliver!* Really! She kissed Thomas's photo as she always did. 'Hello, love, it's a gorgeous day,' she said.

Dot groaned when Jessica walked into the still-empty waiting room. 'How *can* you look like that?' she asked, 'after last night?'

Jessica grinned. 'Like what?'

'Well—radiant, I suppose you'd call it. Well slept and rested and at peace with the world, which I definitely am not.' She held her hand to her drooping head.

Radiant! And at peace with the world! Did her new-found centre of calm really show that much?

'Headache?' she asked Dot, her voice sympathetic.

Dot winced. 'The mother and father of a headache,' she said bitterly. 'And don't tell me it's my own fault—I know it.'

Jessica patted her hand. 'I'll get you something from the first-aid cupboard.'

Jane, who'd been talking on the phone, finished her call. She raised her eyebrows at Jessica. 'It's always the same. She can drink anyone under the table, but does she suffer for it the next day.'

'I don't think I want to live,' moaned Dot.

'You'll have to. Time to open up,' Jane pointed out. 'Your public needs you.'

On cue, there was a loud hammering at the street door and a man's voice shouting for help in a mixture of English and some other language.

'My son, he cannot breathe, he swallow something,' Jessica and Jane made out, as they deactivated the alarm and began unlocking the complicated system of locks and bolts on the double doors.

'I'll see if either of the doctors are in,' called Dot, her headache seeming magically to have disappeared.

'Come in, Mr Patel,' said Jane breathlessly, as the doors slid open and a man almost fell in. He was carrying an infant, who looked to be about two years old.

'Prakash,' he said, 'he needs doctor, he's choking.'

With some difficulty, Jessica prised the baby out of his arms. 'I'm a nurse,' she said firmly. 'Tell me what happened—what did he swallow?'

'Button, a button off my sleeve.' The father pointed to his jacket. There were two other small buttons there.

Jessica sat down on the nearest chair. She rested her arm on her knees, laid the child along it with his head tipped downwards and gave him five sharp slaps on his back.

From experience she knew that sometimes an obstruction flew or fell out of the mouth at this point. But this time there was nothing. She turned the boy over onto his back, and with one finger carefully examined his mouth to feel if the object was still lodged in his throat. There was something, but it was too far back for her to reach. If she tried she might push it further down the tiny throat and cause damage.

The baby remained blue. The father was half praying, half shouting at Jessica to save his son. The patients who had followed Mr Patel in were crowding round. Jessica told them sharply to move back and asked Jane to fetch the emergency oxygen kit from the treatment room. While issuing these instructions, she placed two fingers at the bottom of the toddler's breastbone, a finger-width below the level of his nipples, and with the fingers of her other hand administered five upward thrusts into his chest.

Prakash made a curious coughing, hiccuping sound. Jessica repeated the thrusting movement with her fingers just below his breastbone. He coughed again and began to struggle. It was his first sign of movement. Mr Patel cried out. Jessica gently eased open the infant's mouth and hooked a small white button from his tongue.

Several things happened in quick succession. Prakash coughed, a rasping cough this time, the blueness began to fade from his face and he started to cry. There was a concerted sigh of relief from the circle of patients, who were edging in again. Jane arrived with the small oxygen kit and, with tears of relief running down his cheeks, Mr Patel tried to hug Prakash.

'Just hang on a minute,' said Jessica firmly but gently to Mr Patel. 'I want to give him a little oxygen, and then one of the doctors will examine his throat to make sure there's no damage done. Just give him a kiss on his forehead, hold his hand and talk to him.'

Mr Patel bent over his son and kissed him with great tenderness on his hairline. Prakash bawled louder than ever, and everyone smiled.

A woman in the crowd said, 'That's the best sound I've heard for a long time.'

There was a murmur of assent and a tangible feeling of relief all round. The baby might have died, but hadn't.

Through tears and smiles Mr Patel said, 'Thank you, thank you, thank you, Nurse. You save my boy.'

Jessica shook her head and felt herself blushing. A glow of happiness stole over her. 'That's what I'm here for,' she murmured.

She stood up, holding the oxygen mask in position a few inches away from the small face. His crying had become sobbing. 'Come on, Mr Patel, we'll go to the treatment room and wait for one of the doctors to come.'

'Will I do?' asked Oliver, suddenly appearing at the back of the interested group still crowded round the centre of the drama.

The patients parted to let him through. Some drifted over to the reception desk to report in.

Oliver stood beside Jessica and with his forefinger smoothed tears from Prakash's tiny cheek. Just as he brushed my tears away, thought Jessica.

He held out his arms. 'Here, let me take him. Tell me what happened,' he said, as they made their way towards the treatment room.

Before Jessica could say a word Mr Patel broke in excitedly. 'She save my boy's life. He swallow a button, couldn't breathe, he was all blue. Nurse got it out—she's very clever lady.' He proffered his upturned hand toward Oliver. The tiny pearl button gleamed against his palm. 'See!'

Oliver glanced at it and grinned at Jessica. She was looking uncomfortable. 'Oh, she's a very clever lady indeed,' he confirmed, as he laid Prakash on the treatment couch. 'We couldn't manage without her. Now, Mr Patel, will you hold Prakash's hand while I have a look at his throat to see if the button's done any damage?'

Prakash made it known, loudly, that he didn't think that a good idea. Jessica, using all her persuasiveness and the bribe of a lollypop to suck when his ordeal was over, eventually managed to get him to open his mouth.

Gently holding down the boy's tongue with a depressor, Oliver shone in a pencil beam of light and examined the reddened throat.

After a minute he stood up and smiled down at the small figure. 'I think,' he said, 'that Daddy must give you lots and lots of ice cream to make your throat better. Oh, and Nurse Friday's lolly, of course.'

Jessica offered the large tin. Prakash chose a red lolly.

'He can have all ice cream in the freezer,' promised Mr Patel. He swept his son off the couch and, with more effusive thanks, departed.

'Thanks to you, Nurse Friday, heroine of the day—' Oliver's eyes gleamed as they met Jessica's '—there goes a very happy patient.'

Jessica dropped the used spatula and some wipes into the bin. Her cheeks reddened. Funny, she thought she was past blushing, yet it had happened several times lately. 'You didn't have to encourage him,' she said dryly. 'He was overdoing the gratitude bit. You know very well that any competent nurse could have done the same.'

'But not, according to what Dot told me, with such speed and sureness. The whole episode apparently only took a minute or so and you didn't bungle once. Removing an obstruction can be tricky. You need a strong nerve and a steady hand, both attributes you clearly possess.' His eyes smiled into hers.

Calmly she smiled back, but her heart was thumping as she turned away to put fresh paper strips on the couch. Dot had said she looked radiant this morning. Well, so did he, if men could look radiant. But she couldn't think of a better word for the way he looked. His lean, lightly tanned face was lit up, his cheek-bones and slightly crooked nose highlighted. And it wasn't her imagination.

She turned back to face him. 'My years in A and E weren't exactly wasted,' she said.

He moved a step forward. 'We should talk, Jess.'

The phone rang.

'Hi,' said Jane brightly. 'Are you ready for business?'

'As of this minute,' replied Jessica.

'Is the boss with you by any chance?'

'He is.'

'Well, will you tell him that he has a whole load of patients champing at the bit?'

Oliver moved to the door. 'Tell Jane that I'm on my way, and please apologise for my late start. See you at lunchtime—we can talk then.'

'No.' It was a firm no. 'Come to the cottage this evening. I'll rustle something up as a thank you for your help on Saturday. You can bring a decent bottle of wine if you feel inclined—I haven't had a chance to stock up on such luxuries. Shall we say seven-thirtyish?'

'Seven-thirtyish,' repeated Oliver, letting himself out of the room.

The corridor was empty. He leaned against the wall and closed his eyes for a moment. Had he just been invited—no—ordered to appear at the cottage by his surgery nurse? Yes! He had.

He grinned. It was unbelievable. Not since he was a small boy, being ordered about by his mother, had a woman ordered him to do anything. Neither, for that matter, since he'd left his medical student days behind him, had any man.

Even Lucinda hadn't dared to order him to do anything. She might think otherwise, but when she got her own way it was because he was happy to go along with her.

Did that make him a chauvinist? Did he feel superior to women? No! He admired most of the women he met in the course of the day. They worked their socks off to keep their families fed and happy. He felt humbled by their achievements. Most of them were bright and intelligent and often well informed about their bodies—whereas the men were largely ignorant.

No, he was definitely no chauvinist, he had no problem with equality between the sexes. But being commanded in a no-nonsense voice to come to dinner by his serene and beautiful nurse, to whom he had recently offered a shoulder to cry on, was astonishing.

She hadn't even enquired if he had a prior appointment—or had she assumed that, if he had, he would break it? No, she wouldn't think like that, she wasn't imperious or arrogant—that was Lucinda's style. She must have assumed, rightly, that if he'd had other things to do that evening he'd have said so.

He shouldered himself away from the wall and made his way to his consulting room. Laughter bubbled up from deep inside him.

He recalled his mother saying, 'You're too clever by half. One day you're going to meet your match.' Had he met his match in Jessica Friday? he wondered as he sat down at his desk and buzzed for his first patient.

Jessica's calm stayed with her as the morning rushed past in a kaleidoscope of physical and emotional problems.

She was getting used to patients presenting with relatively minor aches, pains, cuts and bruises, which were quickly dealt with, then suddenly finding herself deep in conversation concerning the *real* problem that had brought them to the surgery.

About half of these were directly, or indirectly, patients in financial difficulties.

Mrs Rita Lang was a case in point. She didn't have an appointment, but had arrived mid-morning complaining of a sprained wrist following a fall.

Dot phoned Jessica. 'Will you see her?' she asked. 'Both Rory and the boss are up to their eyes. I don't think it's badly hurt—she keeps waving it about. Probably all it needs is a bandage. In fact, I'm surprised she's come in, she doesn't usually worry us for something like this. I think she's got something on her mind, and wants to talk about it.'

As usual, Dot was right.

Jessica had hardly begun examining Mrs Lang's wrist when it all came pouring out. Her husband had been made redundant. How were they going to pay the rent? Her greatest fear was that the children would be taken from her because they wouldn't have a roof over their heads.

'No,' Jessica said firmly, gently massaging the painful wrist with an analgesic ointment to soothe and bring out the bruise. 'No one is going to do that. You're not going to be homeless. Somewhere along the line you can get help to pay the rent. You must go to the Social Security office and talk to them.'

'My husband won't let me do that. He's never been out of work before, and he's ashamed. He'll collect his unemployment, but he says anything else is scrounging.'

Jessica was surprised. She was used to older people being reluctant to ask for what they considered 'charity', but Mr Lang could only be in his forties, not old enough to think that way. It was refreshing to hear, but it didn't stop Mrs Lang worrying about how to pay the rent.

Jessica was lost for a moment, and then said, 'Are you working?'

'Yes, but only part time. My earnings wouldn't keep us in food.'

'Could you work longer hours while your husband's at home to look after the children?'

Rita looked doubtful. 'I work at McDonald's, and though they're busy all year round it does drop off a bit at the end of the season and there may not be any hours going. Anyway, like a lot of men, Dave isn't all that good with the kids.'

Jessica clamped her lips together. So Dave had a high moral code but that didn't include sharing chores with his wife. She pulled herself up. She musn't criticise, it wouldn't help.

'Have you told him how worried you are about the rent?'

'I mentioned it once, but he got pretty angry.' Rita's eyes filled with tears. She blinked them back, looked down at her lap and muttered, 'He says if I managed the housekeeping better, we wouldn't have a problem.'

Jessica's antennae were suddenly alert. How angry had he got, and had his anger any connection with Rita's fall? Was he a violent man? Were there other bruises? Should she question Rita more? She looked at the bent head. No, the poor woman wasn't fit to be questioned any more at the moment. And it would be a good idea, before doing that, to have a word with Oliver and get his opinion.

He probably knew the family history and could give a lead as to what action to take. Jessica carefully finished bandaging the sprained wrist and covered it with a Tubigrip support bandage. 'I'd like to see you in a few days' time,' she said, 'just to check that it's going on all right. Rest it as much as possible. You can't be too careful with even a minor sprain.'

That wasn't strictly true, of course. There wasn't any need to look at the wrist again, but she wanted to get Rita back to the surgery after she'd spoken to Oliver.

Rita agreed to make an appointment for one morning the following week. But she gave

Jessica an odd look as she said goodbye and thanked her for treating her wrist, and Jessica knew that she'd seen through the ploy. Not that it mattered. She'd agreed to come, and that was important.

Jessica made a note to speak to Oliver at the first opportunity—tonight, perhaps, when he came to dinner? Her calm was shaken a little at the thought of spending the evening with him, but she took a few deep breaths and was back on course.

She went through to the waiting room and called in her next patient. Warren Fox, a sallow, stringy lad of twenty with several boils on his back, and had come in for dressings. In spite of an umbrella of antibiotics, they hadn't improved much since Jessica had cleaned and dressed them a week before. She wasn't surprised. He appeared to live on a diet of chips, crisps and lager, and he smoked heavily.

It would fall on deaf ears, but she tried once more to explain that eating fruit or fresh vegetables would help the boils clear up.

As always, he shrugged and said, 'Yeah, well…'

Her next two patients were both in for iron injections. It was slow, tedious business which could be painful if not given properly deep into the muscle, without staining the surrounding skin.

Both patients had praised her for giving them a painless injection. It still gave her a boost when patients went away feeling happy with her efforts.

Her last patient was Barry Woods.

What was he doing back again? Another fight? Only last week his mother had brought him in with a cut just beneath one eye, which had been pinking up nicely and swelling rapidly. He'd been attacked, Isla said, by a bigger boy. And the proverbial pigs might fly, thought Jessica, catching a knowing gleam in the boy's good eye.

If ever there was a bully boy, Barry was it.

The big, scruffy twelve-year-old shuffled reluctantly towards her, trailed by his mother. He was holding a wad of bloody tissues to his chin.

'Hello, Barry, been in the wars again?' Jessica ushered the pair along the corridor and into the treatment room.

''Sright,' he mumbled, his mouth stiff. He clearly found it painful to talk.

'Let me have a look, then, love.' Carefully Jessica eased the tissues away from his chin. Blood streamed from a deep cut. She clamped clean tissues to the wound. He'd been hit really hard by a fist like a rock—a man's fist? Did his jaw look a bit odd? Could it be broken? 'This is a really nasty one, Barry. I'm going to get one of the doctors to have a look at it. Hold that in place.' She placed his hand over the tissues.

Barry shook his head and mumbled something.

'Sorry, I can't understand you, Barry.'

'He don't want t'see the doctors, Nurse. Can't you stitch him up like last time?' Isla was twitching with anxiety.

'Sorry, the cut's too deep, and I think his jaw might be broken—not badly, maybe, but it may need attention. He might have to have an X-ray at the hospital.'

Why were both mother and son so uptight, as if they had something to hide? Was there another aggressive man in the background? Jessica picked up the phone and got through to Reception.

Oliver arrived a few minutes later. He paused in the doorway, his eyes sweeping over the trolley and the bowl holding the bloody tissues and then to Barry.

'So, what happened this time, Barry? Was it your supplier? Weren't you pushing hard enough?' In two strides he crossed the room and stood in front of the boy.

Pushing! A supplier! No wonder mother and son had looked scared. Obviously Oliver knew them well. Even so, Jessica was surprised at his reaction. He so seldom showed his feelings in front of the patients. Now he didn't sound particularly angry, just exasperated and rather sad, but Barry looked terrified. All his swagger had left him.

He mumbled something inarticulate.

Mrs Woods put her hand on Oliver's sleeve. 'Please, Doctor, don't turn him in. He won't have no more to do with them, promise, and it's only a bit of pot, no hard stuff.'

'You keep on promising, Isla, but nothing ever comes of it. The so-called soft drugs are a beginning. For Barry's sake, and the other kids he pushes to, we've got to get the authorities involved. But we'll talk about that later. Right now I want to see what damage has been done—fill me in, please, Nurse.' He looked across at Jessica, his mouth relaxing into a tender smile.

The smile shook her. Her insides churned. She steadied her fingers, and lifted the soiled tissues from Barry's jaw. The bleeding was beginning to ease up.

'I think it's going to need a couple of deep sutures as well as superficial ones—that's why I thought you should see it. I also think that his jaw's slightly out of alignment and there may be a hairline fracture.'

Their eyes met briefly. His grey ones telegraphed warmth and admiration, before he lowered them to examine the cut. 'Yes, you're right, but I think I can manage it under a local.' He stood back and searched Barry's face, then gently ran his fingers along his jawline. 'And you're right about the jaw. We'll have to get it X-rayed.'

'Does that mean he'll have to go to the hospital?' asked Mrs Woods in a wobbly voice, clutching her bag with tight fingers.

'Yes, I'm afraid it does. We'll make him as comfortable as we can, but I'd rather he didn't go on the bus. Perhaps we can arrange for one of our volunteer drivers to take you. We'll see what can be done.'

Half an hour later, Mrs Woods and Barry, with his cut stitched and jaw bandaged to hold it still, were collected by a volunteer driver and left for the hospital.

Jessica began tidying up the debris and wished that Oliver would go away. She was acutely conscious of him standing, watching her. Her deep, newly discovered calm was still there. Strong though her attraction to him was, he couldn't reach that. But she had geared herself for tonight's meeting, and until then she wanted to keep her distance.

'Barry didn't need a car,' she said. 'He could have made it all right on the bus. Is this some sort of VIP treatment for kids on drugs? Is it meant to make them open up? I don't think he or any of the druggies I met in A and E would be very impressed if that was offered to them as a sweetener.'

She glanced at Oliver. He looked very re-laxed, leaning against the door, all six feet something of him, his wide shoulders emphas-ised by the blue cable-knit sweater he was wearing. He was indecently handsome and so very nice with it—a young girl's dream of a perfect catch. But, she reminded herself briskly, you're not a young girl, but a woman of thirty-four, and you know that there's no such thing as a perfect catch.

Oliver snorted a laugh. 'A sweetener, is that what you thought? I'm not that naïve. Anyway, he's not a user, he's a pusher in a very small way.'

Jessica shuddered. Of all people, dealers and suppliers were those she hated most. Users were often more to be pitied than blamed. It was almost impossible for them to get off drugs once they'd started. But the suppliers who kept them going were something else— and one as young as Barry, supplying his schoolmates. Why on earth didn't Oliver report him to the police? By not doing so, he was compounding a crime.

She said through clenched teeth, 'Then why a car?'

'Because his mum hadn't got the bus fare. Didn't you notice how her fingers tightened round her bag when the hospital was mentioned?'

He didn't miss a trick. 'I did, but I thought it was simply fear of going to hospital. A lot of people are scared stiff.'

'True, but I assure you that's not the case with our Isla. Between her husband and Barry, she's spent half her rotten life in hospitals, poor woman.'

'I thought she was a single mother or divorced or something, since she didn't mention a husband.'

He shook his head. 'No, her husband's in prison—again—though he'd not been long out. Barry hasn't had much of a role model.'

Jessica experienced a twinge of doubt. Was she being too hard on the boy? 'Where on earth does he get the money to buy supplies?'

'Don't ask,' said Oliver gloomily. 'As far as I know, it's only marijuana and the boy loves his mum in his own way, contributes toward the housekeeping. Isla thinks the world of him, depends on him. She's one of those women who needs a man about the house. If it weren't for Barry, she'd have probably had a succession of unsavoury men supposedly looking after her.'

Jessica made a moue of distaste. 'I know, I've met them. It's incredible how in this day and age so many women are totally dependent on men. It's almost indecent.'

Oliver said softly, 'Do you really think that, Jess? You sound as if you despise them. Can't you find it in your heart to feel just a little

sorry for women who are weaker than you?'
There was a note of surprise and disappointment in his voice. In other words, what had
happened to his perfect nurse with an abun-
dance of TLC for all her patients?

In the act of putting utensils into the steriliser, she froze. It was the first time he had
sounded critical of her, and she didn't like it
one bit. Colour came and went in her face. She
musn't let him see that he had disturbed her,
almost but not quite reaching down into her
still centre of calm.

'Of course I feel sorry for them, desperately
sorry, but I wish they would find the guts to
manage without a man, especially the sort of
man they seem to go for.'

'Have you ever had to manage without a
man, or someone to support you?'

'Of course I have…' She stopped. Someone
to support you! Her parents had always been
there for her when she had needed them most.
'Oh.' She covered her mouth with her fingers
for a moment. 'What you mean is that a lot of
these women haven't got *anyone* behind them
and that finding a man is their best option.'

'Exactly. Oh, some of them can't live without sex, but a lot of them just want a man

around for protection. They're terribly vulner-able, Jess, and feel even more so without a man. Even if they end up keeping him finan-cially, as they so often do. The fact of having a man lends them a sort of cachet with their neighbours, boosts their self-respect. It's tough for those women out there.'

Jessica spread her hands in a gesture of helplessness. 'How dumb can I get?' She burst out in disgust. 'I've been nursing all these years in a rough area, and hadn't cottoned onto that simple fact. Just feeling sorry for them isn't enough. It's patronising, isn't it?'

Oliver shook his head, crossed the room and took her hands in his. 'I've never heard you sound patronising to anybody,' he said, 'but understanding is important. You don't see pa-tients long enough in A and E, but you learn a lot in a practice like this, you get to know whole families. Imagine being on your own with two or three kids trapped in a flat a mile high, unsavoury neighbours and no adult com-pany. Wouldn't you welcome anyone—?'

'Don't!' Jessica exploded. 'It doesn't bear thinking about.' She looked up into his austere face. 'How come you understand these things so well? It must be a world away from what

you're used to. You're well educated and, like
me, you must have always had support from a
loving family and no real financial worries. So
how do you do it, Oliver?'

He squeezed her hands tighter, and then let
them go and stepped away from her. She
couldn't see into his eyes, but a strange expression flitted across his face, which hardened
and saddened.

'Ah, thereby hangs a tale,' he said dryly, 'to
which one day you may be privy.' He raised
one hand in a farewell gesture and opened the
door with the other. 'See you tonight, your
place, seven-thirty as commanded.' He disappeared into the corridor, closing the door quietly behind him.

CHAPTER NINE

OLIVER arrived as two silvery strokes, chiming the half-hour, rang out on the wall clock in the hall.

'Bang on time,' said Jessica, throwing the door open wide and hoping he wouldn't hear her thundering heartbeats. Pull yourself together woman. Of course he can't hear them.

Silhouetted by an early moon shining on the still waters of the estuary, his well-shaped head and wide shoulders were thrown into bas-relief. The amber porch light burnished his black hair. The familiar smell of him, clean and soapy tinged with antiseptic, wafted to her, mingling with the salty sea smell.

She breathed in deeply. 'Please, do come in.' She sounded like a nervous society hostess—and felt like it.

He stepped in, filling the hall, dwarfing her. 'Nice piece. Eighteenth century?' He nodded towards the clock.

The vibes, already sparking, didn't have far to travel. They seemed to leap across the small

space between them. Jessica tingled from top
to toe, and managed a breathy, 'Yes, legacy
from my godmother—she was something of a
collector.'

Oliver handed her a dark, gold-topped bottle. 'This had better go in the fridge,' he said.

'Again!' she exclaimed. 'Champagne.'

'The real stuff this time—thought we might
need it.' Her bob of fine silver-blonde hair curtained her eyes as she bent her head to examine
the label. He wanted to stroke it, sift it through
his fingers, test its silkiness.

She raised her face and her brown eyes sparkled with dots of gold as they caught the light.
She grinned. 'My word, I'm not a connoisseur,
but even I know this costs the earth.' She tilted
her head to one side.

Like a beautiful, inquisitive bird, he thought.

'Why do you think we might need it?'

'I'm not sure how the evening's going to
go—are you, Jess?' It was his turn to look
quizzical. 'I suggested we might talk over a
ploughman's at the pub, but you hyped it up
with this invitation to supper.'

Jessica met his eyes square on. They're brilliant tonight, she noted, not grey but a silvery
blue. 'Yes, I did, didn't I?' She grinned again,

but this time there was a faint flush in her cheeks. 'Almost ordered you to come in fact.'

Oliver hoped she wouldn't apologise for that.

She didn't, but wrinkled her nose and sniffed. 'I'd better check the oven.' She whirled round and rushed through the sitting room to the kitchen.

He followed slowly, admiring her neat, black-velveted buttocks beneath the sloppy white sweater, catching a whiff of her delicate perfume, noting the touches she'd added to the room since he'd been there on Saturday—colourful cushions on the sofa and easy chairs, prints on the walls, a bowl of flowers and a tulip desk lamp on the bureau, and a bright wool rug in front of the open fireplace, where an apple-scented log fire sparked and blazed behind a wire guard.

At the far end of the room a round, polished table was laid for a meal, with several glasses by each place setting. There was a range of cutlery on either side of the table mats, and snow-white napkins in polished wooden rings. A table laid to perfection, women's magazine stuff.

So it was dinner rather than supper.

'I'd have worn a black tie had I known it was to be a formal do,' he teased, as he stood in the doorway opening into the kitchen. 'There's only one thing missing to complete an elegant tête-à-tête setting for two.'

Jessica, crouching on her haunches in front of the Aga, looked up at him, her face startled and flushed. 'Oh, Lord, what have I forgotten?'

'Candles?' he suggested, smiling, his eyebrows raised.

She turned back to the Aga, pulled out a casserole dish with oven-gloved hands and lifted the lid. Aromatic steam drifted across the kitchen. Still crouching, she stretched up with one hand and waved it over the worktop.

'This what you're looking for?' Oliver handed her a large serving spoon.

'Thanks.' She stirred the casserole, replaced the lid and slid it back into the oven. On the shelf above was a tray of golden potatoes roasting to crisp perfection. She moved them about with the spoon and slurped a little oil over them. 'They tend to stick if you're not careful,' she said, closing the oven door and standing up.

She came face to face with Oliver, standing only inches away. If she breathed in deeply…

She glanced down at her white sweater—it still hung loosely over her breasts, though they suddenly felt full and taut.

'So why no candles?'

She risked a small intake of breath. 'I didn't think the occasion warranted it. After all, we're only going to talk.' *Only going to talk!* That was an understatement as if she could muster the courage, she was going to quiz him as he had quizzed her on Saturday. She had bared her soul to him, let him into her heart's secret, and it had opened up a whole new beginning for her. Now she wanted to do the same for him, teach him to unwind. She wanted to offer him a shoulder to cry on, or, better still, a soft breast.

Humour, and some other expression that she couldn't fathom, flickered across his face.

'Ah—so we're not talking a romantic dinner for two.'

'Of course not,' she said sharply, putting the vegetables into the colander but not placing it over the pan of nearly boiling water. 'Would you, please, pour the wine for our starters? The dry white—it's in the fridge.'

He stood with the bottle in his hand. 'Is it business, then?'

She didn't comment but took two dishes from the fridge to carry them through to the table. 'Starters,' she said. 'I hope you'll like it—melon and mango with a squeeze of lime juice and a touch of ginger.'

'You sound like a TV cook.' He poured the wine and returned the bottle to the fridge.

'And you were being deliberately obtuse. You know very well it's not business,' Jessica said, as he sat down opposite her.

They both picked up their glasses and clinked them together.

Oliver sipped his wine. 'Nice! So, if it's not business and not romance...' He was half smiling, but his eyes were intense.

Jessica tasted a piece of mango, and nodded her head. 'Try yours,' she suggested.

'You're procrastinating, aren't you?' He speared a piece of melon.

'Yes—let's wait till we've eaten,' she said firmly. You were right. Bringing the champagne was a brilliant idea—we are going to need it.'

He said softly. 'It's only me you'll be talking to, Jess.'

Only him! Each day the vibes rippling back and forth between them had been tightening.

What had started as the faint pull of physical attraction had grown into something fathoms deep. He had only to walk into a room for her spine to tingle, the hairs on the back of her neck to stand up. And she sensed that it was the same for him. They had not spoken overtly of love, but they were immersed in it. It folded itself around them.

They made light, frothy conversation as they ate—Oliver with relish and compliments, Jessica pickily and hoping he was really enjoying it. They talked of holidays, past and possibly to come, though neither had made plans for the following year.

'One wonders if it's worth it.' Oliver sipped the red wine complementing the casserole. 'What with cancelled and delayed flights and the aggro of getting to the airport to start with. I'm seriously thinking of something nearer home this year, Scotland, perhaps, the highlands and islands, avoiding the motorways.'

'That's where we used to go when I was a child.' There was a dreamy look in Jessica's eyes. 'Dad was the junior partner in the practice, and with four kids he and Mum couldn't afford anything fancy. There weren't all the package holidays around that there are now, so we caravanned. It was a big caravan with an extension tent, which was our living room and where the boys slept.'

Oliver, happy to see her relaxed, urged her on to tell more. 'The boys?'

'Twins, Nick and Ned. They're five years younger than I am. Ally, my sister, is three years younger. It was great. We camped on Skye for several years, near a lovely sandy beach, with a little outcrop with a rowan tree jutting out into the sea. The beach was hard to get to down a difficult, bendy lane, so we had it almost to ourselves. Occasionally other people showed up, but they never stayed long.'

She sipped her wine and smiled at Oliver, and received such a tender smile in return that she wished there *were* candles on the table. It was that sort of dinner. Romance was almost crackling in the air around them.

She took a deep breath and said in a rush, 'We had such adventures. It was like something out of the *Famous Five* books, with exciting things happening every day. And Mum and Dad were marvellous. They joined in sometimes, but just to have them there was magic. They were available, they made it safe.'

Oliver pictured four silver-haired children in shorts and sandals, clambering over the outcrop, which must have seemed like a mountain to them.

'And I bet you were leader of the pack,' he said softly.

'Of course, I was the oldest,' she said with dignity. 'What about you, Oliver? What are your best childhood memories of holidays?'

At a guess, he would have travelled to exotic places with his wealthy parents, with a nanny to look after him—certainly nothing as humble as a caravan holiday. Perhaps they had a yacht, not a modest one like Dad's runabout, but a big one, with sleek, elegant lines and a professional crew.

He was a long time answering. He looked suddenly pale and pinched, his jaw prominent and his eyes distant and full of pain.

She stretched a hand across the table and touched his cheek. 'Oliver?'

He flinched, and forced his eyes to focus on her.

'Sorry, daydreaming, childhood memories and all that.'

'Not happy ones?'

He smiled, almost a normal smile, just as his voice was almost, but not quite, normal.

'For various reasons, holidays weren't on the agenda when I was a child. Just the occasional day at the beach, that was about it. But, there, that's another story, and it's you—us—we're going to talk about, isn't it?'

'That's what you said before—that's another story. What other story, Oliver? And why does it make you look so sad?' She felt bold asking it, but she had to. She wanted to help, take the sadness out of his voice and his eyes. That was what this evening was about.

He said. 'I'd rather talk about you, Jess.'

She shook her head. 'No. We've talked about me. You know the most important thing about me, about Thomas. There's nothing else to tell except the trivia of everyday things. I suggested having dinner here tonight so that we could talk about you. After all, you were the one who said we should talk.'

He frowned. 'About *us*, Jess, not me.'

'Why not you?' asked Jess, her voice brisk. 'Let's stop pussyfooting around.' It was her turn to frown. 'If there's to be an "us" then we should start with a level playing field. Something's bothering you, makes you look sad. You hide behind steely eyes just as I was hiding behind a cool, detached façade. But that's not you, Oliver, any more than my ice maiden image was the real me.'

Oliver met her eyes across the table. 'You're serious, aren't you, about wanting to know?'

'Deadly serious. I'm not quite sure what you mean by ''us'', but if it means getting to know each other better, then let's start doing that right now.'

Oliver stood up abruptly. 'Could we sit more comfortably?'

Jessica nodded and moved across to the leather chesterfield taking her red wine with her.

Oliver sat down beside her, not in the far corner but so that his thigh, warm and muscular, was touching hers.

He started abruptly. 'I've been attracted to you, Jess, since the day you came for your interview.' His voice was very matter-of-fact. 'Don't quite know why. You're beautiful and sexy and any man in his right mind would fall for you, hook, line and sinker, as my Dad would say, just as I did. But that was hormones and stuff, nothing like this feeling that's been growing in me.'

With his head back, he tossed the remainder of the red wine down his throat as if it were water.

Jessica watched his strong throat muscles and Adam's apple working rhythmically. She wanted to kiss the smooth, taut flesh and brush her lips over the glistening dark hairs disappearing into the neckline of his sweater.

A mixture of calm yet tingling excitement washed over her. She felt like another woman, not the cool, conventional Jessica Friday. It was weird. She feasted on his words. 'Were you really attracted to me from the word go?'

'Yes. When I saw those gorgeous legs of yours as they emerged from the car, they knocked me for six, and when I saw the rest of you... Wow.'

Colour crept up into her cheeks—did he really think she had gorgeous legs?

He waved his empty glass about. 'But, like I said, that was only a physical reaction...this feeling...' he put his free hand over the region of his heart '...is quite different. I've never experienced anything like it before, it comes from somewhere deep down inside me. It's painful, and it makes me breathless sometimes.'

Oliver put down his empty glass, took her half-full one and placed it beside his on the table. Turning to face her, he cupped her chin in both his hands and outlined her lips with his thumbs.

Jess shivered. Had he really said that he'd never experienced it before? A sophisticated man of the world who must have known many women—who knew Lucinda Grant.

She had to ask. 'Not even with Lucinda?'

He looked startled and fierce for a moment, his eyes suddenly pewter grey. He dropped his hands from her face.

'*Never* with Lucinda. How could you think that? She's a friend, that's all, and even our friendship is going through a rocky patch at the moment. She has a quick, intelligent mind and can be a fun person to go out with.'

And comes with the right sort of connections, Jessica thought nastily.

She squashed the thought but couldn't leave it alone. 'And she doesn't look too bad either,' she said dryly, wishing she hadn't thrown Lucinda's name into the conversation. Why must she spoil the evening by being bitchy? Jealousy wasn't normally in her make-up, so why couldn't she leave well alone? No mystery. Because she loved him and the thought of anyone else…

'Yes, she's a stunner, there is that.' His voice was as dry as hers, his mouth curled at one corner. Frowning, he said, 'I seem to remember having a similar conversation with you about Lucinda before, and I thought I'd made myself clear on our relationship then.' His nostrils flared. He was at his most arrogant.

Jessica drew on her reserve of calm and courage. She could only be truthful. She met his eyes boldly. 'Yes, you did, and I accepted it—still do. I guess I just wanted to hear you say it again.'

This time it was she who cupped *his* chin and pleaded. 'Oliver, I seem to need tons of reassurance. It has to do with this feeling of having known you for ever. Like you, I've never experienced it before. It's fantastic, and a bit frightening, and I can't believe it's happened to me.' Her voice dropped to a trembling whisper.

'In the conventional sense we hardly know each other, but time doesn't seem to matter. I want to build on what we've got…this feeling. I can't explain it but I'm afraid of losing it...and you,' she added in a voice even less than a whisper. 'That's why I need to know what's bugging you, and I need to know it before our relationship moves forward. I took a chance once, and lost so much. It changed my life. I'm not going to do it again.'

Oliver took hold of her wrists and, easing her hands away from his chin, kissed both her palms. Then she was in his arms, cradled on his lap.

He kissed the crown of her head, her forehead, her lips. They were gentle, sweet, reassuring kisses.

'You know I would never hurt you,' he said.

'Then, tell me where you're coming from. Why you almost seem to be two personalities. Why you seem at home in Berkley Square and equally at home in Arundel Street, or in my little cottage. How is it you seem to understand what it is to be poor when you're...very comfortably off? You're a distinguished consultant in the private sector, yet you work incredibly hard in the NHS. You don't need to, so what drives you?'

'There's nothing strange in that. Many consultants work in both sectors. I think most of us feel that we owe the NHS for our training.'

She nodded. 'That's true, but you do it with such...devotion. You do more than is demanded of you and the patients think the world of you, especially those in Arundel Street dependent on the NHS.'

His cheeks reddened. Jessica smiled. 'You're blushing,' she said.

Oliver shrugged. 'The NHS was created for people who couldn't pay for health care and, in spite of private insurance, there are many people who still rely on it. Believe me, I know that only too well. My family is a case in point.'

Jessica stiffened with surprise. He nuzzled her hair and brushed a kiss across her lips.

'My parents both worked on the Castle Estate on the Devon-Cornwall border. My father was a general farm worker and my mother worked in the dairy, producing the now famous Castle cream and cheese.' His mouth twisted sardonically. 'Sounds idyllic, doesn't it, storybook stuff? In fact, forty odd years ago they worked long hours for a pittance.

'They still live in the tied terraced cottage which was part of their wages. But they loved it, cared for it, did repairs that, by right, their landlord should have done. They bought it out of the estate when it was being split up some years ago.'

Jess had a flash of inspiration. 'You bought it for them, Oliver, didn't you?' She kissed his cheek.

He looked sad. 'It was one of the rare occasions that they let me do anything for them, Jess, in spite of all they did for me. I was lucky enough to win a scholarship to a rather distinguished old public school where I was a boarder. You know, there are a hell of a lot of things that a scholarship doesn't cover. Somehow my parents managed, bought me books and uniform, everything I needed.'

She didn't speak at once. Her mind was seething with questions. Because she, like the rest of the staff, had assumed that he came from a privileged background, the truth took some digesting. It explained how he was able to blend in with Arundel Street and identify with the patients there. And no wonder he'd known about the back lobby where he'd hung his wet mac on Saturday. His parents lived in a cottage like her own two up and one down.

What the brief history hadn't explained was why he'd been, to say the least, reticent about his background. Was he ashamed of his humble beginnings? She couldn't believe that—he spoke about them with such affection. In fact, he obviously admired his parents for what they had done for him.

She slid out of his arms and off his lap and crouched in front of the fire, throwing on more logs. With her back still to him, she said, 'Why have you kept your background quiet? I know you're not ashamed of it, so why?'

'Not my idea, it was my parents'. It started when I went to medical school. I know today's young people would find it hard to believe, but the attitude nearly thirty years ago was different. The cracks were beginning to show, but doctors for the most part didn't come from working-class families. My parents are extremely old-fashioned. They thought that it would hold me back if it was widely known that I came from simple labouring stock.'

He grunted. 'Their words, not mine. I've never gone out of my way to conceal my working-class origins, but no one's ever questioned them. I've got the right accent, wear the right clothes, there's no contest really.' He reached out and touched her shoulder.

'Jess, is it important to you that I'm not what I might appear to be?'

She swivelled round to face him, her face red from the heat of the fire. She was indignant. 'Of course not, but I'm sorry you didn't tell me before, just as I'm sorry you didn't tell me that you were from Devon. If your people are near the border, they can't be far from my parents. It would have been…friendly to have told me.'

'Yes, you're dead right. Not only friendly but more honest. In my defence I can only say that I have got used to being reticent, it's become natural to me. I have a circle of acquaintances and a handful of casual friends, but no one in whom I would wish to confide.'

Jessica fought down a desperate desire to ask if that included Lucinda.

Oliver, reading her mind, said softly, 'And that includes Lucinda.' He stood up and took her in his arms. 'Jess, only *you*…' his fine mouth twisted into a sardonic smile '…know my secret. If only Mum and Dad would believe that things have changed… I only wish…'

Jess tilted back her head and looked into his eyes. 'There's something else, isn't there?'

'Yes, but I can't say more now. Please, trust me a little longer.' He hugged her close for a moment, then stepped away and held her at arm's length. 'Can you bear to do that, Jess?'

Anything, she thought, if it would take away that pain in his eyes. 'Yes, but don't keep me waiting long.'

'Not a minute more than I have to.'

He looked tired and haggard and incredibly sad. 'Go home,' Jess murmured. 'Have a good night's sleep. All being well, we'll talk again tomorrow.'

'Let me stay and help clear up.' He waved his hand at the table.

She ushered him through the door into the hall. 'No way,' she said firmly, opening the front door. 'Go to bed, Oliver. Things will look better tomorrow.'

CHAPTER TEN

JESSICA was working at Arundel Street the following morning and Oliver was giving a lecture to medical students at Porthampton University. After all that had happened the previous evening, this gave her a welcome break before meeting Oliver when she went on duty at two o'clock at Berkley House.

Arriving for duty, she found that there was no time for embarrassment or explanation. Oliver was in the staff parking area, slinging an overnight bag into the boot of his car.

He strode across as she pulled up.

She let down the window and shivered. Today's October sunshine held no warmth.

He leaned on the sill, resting his chin on his hands, near enough for her to inhale the familiar scent of him. The lines about his mouth were marked, his eyebrows drawn together in a frown, his eyes flinty grey and anxious.

'Sorry about this, Jess. I'd hoped we'd have time to talk more today, but I've got to dash—

my father's had a stroke. I'll be away for a couple of days, maybe longer.'

His voice was brisk and unemotional and would have sounded uncaring to someone who didn't know him. But to Jessica the briskness represented the tight hold he had on his emotions.

Until last night he'd hardly mentioned his parents, but from what he'd said she knew that he held them in very special regard, more than simply loving them. Knowing this, she could guess at the anguish he was going through.

'Oh, Oliver, I'm so sorry. Do you know how severe the stroke is?'

'No, the ambulance arrived as my mother was ringing me. I didn't have a chance to speak to the GP, a locum whom I don't know. I'll find out more when I get to the hospital.'

Jessica laid a hand on his where it rested on the sill, and fancied she felt it tremble. 'I do hope all goes well, Oliver. So much can be done for stroke victims these days, especially if treated early.'

It was a silly thing to say since Oliver knew that, but experience told her that even experts needed reassurance where friends or relatives were concerned. Fear and concern for their loved ones often made them as helpless as lay people.

He dropped a kiss on her hand. 'Bless you,' he murmured. 'I'll keep in touch. There's a note on your desk. There are a few people I want you to see.'

'Will they mind seeing me instead of you? This isn't Arundel Street. Your patients here expect to see the big cheese himself.'

His mouth quirked at the corner. 'On this occasion, tough. Don't worry, Rachel's notified them and they're quite happy to be in your hands. With the exception of Mrs Peters, they're all patients you've seen before. In an emergency, get in touch with the Nightingale, or ring me, I've left my parents' number on the note if you can't get me on my mobile.'

He poked his head through the open window and firmly kissed her on her lips, then turned and walked smartly back to his own car, his shoulders very square, his long legs eating up the strip of gravelled drive between the cars.

She put her fingers to her lips to seal in the kiss, to savour it. Her stomach churned, her pulses hammered, she shivered convulsively. There had been something special about that kiss. There had been no need for words—it had been a kiss full of promise.

Jessica put the kiss, the tenderness in his eyes, which had briefly masked his anxiety, and his hand, which had trembled beneath her own, out of her mind and concentrated on work.

The note was a brief list of the patients he wanted her to see—two antenatal, one postnatal, all previously booked. He wanted blood, pre-eclampsia and glucose urine tests and a general progress report on both the antenatals and a general check-up on the postnatal mother and baby. He'd filled in the details on the appropriate forms for the tests, and had instructed her to make sure they reached the lab that afternoon.

A fourth patient had been booked in—Lady Lyons—for a varicose ulcer to be re-dressed.

The note was professional and to the point, but there was a footnote.

Jess, sorry about the baby emphasis, but I know you'll cope. Leaving everything in your caring, capable hands. Field any med calls that might come in. Use my consulting room, it will give you a bit of clout. Will keep you posted. Oliver.

Feeling like a squatter, she moved into his consulting room. The interphone jangled. It was Rachel. It was reassuring to hear her voice.

'You've missed the boss,' she drawled. 'He's had to—'

'I know,' Jessica interrupted. 'I met him in the car park. His father's had a stroke.'

'He was here, talking to me, when the phone rang. Poor man, he was absolutely poleaxed. I've heard the phrase ''green round the gills'' but I've never seen it happen before. And that's exactly what happened to him.'

'Yes, he looked pretty shaken when I saw him. But, then, if he's as close to his parents as I am to mine, I'm not surprised. I'd be devastated if anything happened to my mum or dad.'

'Lucky you.' Rachel's voice was brittle. 'My parents are never in one place long enough, or together enough, for me to get to know them. The first I'll know if either of them breaks their neck, skydiving, is when I read the obituary in *The Times*.'

'Oh, Rachel... I'm so sorry.' Poor little rich girl. It explained a lot about the sophisticated, fun-loving woman with a succession of men behind her.

Like Oliver, she'd rarely mentioned her parents. It seems that we all have secrets, Jessica thought. An image of baby Thomas flashed into her mind, so vivid that she could smell his milky softness, feel the yielding flesh of his cheek when she kissed him.

Her fingers went white round the receiver. The front doorbell pealed loudly in Reception.

'That'll be your first patient,' breathed Rachel, sounding relieved.

'Mr and Mrs Fawkes,' she announced, moments later.

Fenella Fawkes was eighteen, a young, bubbly eighteen. Married six months ago, she was thrilled to be sixteen weeks pregnant. Jessica had first met her some weeks ago when Oliver had examined her to confirm her pregnancy.

Her husband, Toby, looked even younger than his wife. Blond and bronzed, he positively bounded into the room—as if he'd just come off the playing fields, thought Jessica, hiding a smile. It was difficult seeing either of them as responsible parents, but appearances could be deceiving, and Toby's presence meant that he wanted to be involved.

Jessica shook their hands and waved them into comfortable chairs. 'Hello, Mrs Fawkes. I'm sorry Dr Pendragon has been called away. I do hope you don't mind me doing this routine check-up.'

'Of course not, as long as you know your stuff, which I'm sure you do or Oliver wouldn't be letting you near me. My pa would kill him. Sorry I won't be seeing Oliver, though. For someone hitting forty he's cool.' She beamed. 'And, please, call me Fen. We'll be seeing a lot of each other over the next few months.'

So Oliver was a family friend. Not that there was anything strange in that. Private practices were usually built on personal contacts. And friend or stranger, Oliver treated all his patients with equal courtesy, and certainly didn't let anything interfere with his clinical judgement.

Jessica smiled. 'Right, a few questions first, and then I'll do an internal, take some blood, weigh you and...'

'And that's that?'

'That's that.'

'So it shouldn't take long. Great! We'll have bags of time to go shopping and raid Pa's account at Hanningworths. Their mother and baby department is a rave.'

Fenella was incredibly relaxed for a first-time mother, and Jessica was able to do the internal examination and take blood easily. Rather touchingly, Toby stood beside his wife and held her hand while Jessica was examining her. He winced when Jessica inserted a needle and drew blood.

'Well, that was a breeze.' Fen slid off the treatment couch and fastened up her designer jeans as far as they would go. She giggled. 'Oxfam, here we come,' she said, straightening her loose silk shirt over her slight bulge.

Jessica eyed the expensive jeans. 'Why Oxfam? You could put them away until after the baby's born. Be a goal to aim for, getting trim enough to wear them.'

Fen giggled again. 'No way,' she said. 'Toby's going to buy me an entirely new wardrobe when this little monster's born, aren't you, Tobe?'

Toby beamed and nodded. 'You bet, nothing's too good for my wife.' He gave her an unselfconcious smacking kiss.

Fen kissed him back. 'I shall put away all my girlie things and go all maternal and mature. I want everyone to know that I'm a mum,' she said. 'And I'm going to be good at it.'

'The best,' said Toby, looking at her as if he could eat her.

Kisses seem to be in fashion this afternoon, thought Jessica. She could empathise. She grinned. 'I believe you. You'll make stunning parents.'

And they would, she thought, tidying up for the next patient. They were like a breath of fresh air. Unusual in this cynical day and age, they were naïve and joyful and in love.

Caroline Winters was also sixteen weeks pregnant and rich, but there the similarity with Fenella ended. She was twenty-five and had mentioned a partner who sounded as if he was a smart, something-in-the-city type. But he hadn't accompanied her when she'd made her first visit to see Oliver to confirm her pregnancy and he wasn't with her now.

But someone should be with her. She looked as if a puff of wind might blow her over. Was she anaemic, or was she always as pale as this?

A quick glance at her notes confirmed that she wasn't anaemic—yet.

Tall, elegant in a drooping lily sort of way, pale and languid, she held out a limp hand to Jessica.

'So kind of you to see me,' she drawled.

Tentatively, Jessica shook the limp hand. 'Not at all,' she said. 'Only too pleased. I'm only sorry that Dr Pendragon isn't here to see you.'

Caroline shrugged. 'Doesn't matter. I find men rather inhibiting, don't you? I'd rather have a woman obstetrician, but Ma said that Dr P's the best and insisted that I see him.'

'He *is* the best,' said Jessica firmly, 'but I shall be examining you from time to time, if that's what you prefer.'

'Oh, I would,' said Caroline, 'please.'

So this seemingly sophisticated creature was shy of men! The question-and-answer session about morning sickness and whether there'd been any show of blood or discharge went quickly enough. Her answers were satisfactory, but the internal examination took some time. Caroline might be languid and laid back on the outside, but was rigid inside. Jessica had to work hard at getting her to relax.

'Everything's fine,' she confirmed as she disposed of her gloves. 'The baby's in the right position, there's a strong heartbeat—everything is as it should be at this stage.'

Caroline smiled wanly. 'Oh, good,' she said, her voice flat.

'And next week you'll be having your scan. There's nothing to be apprehensive about, it's normal procedure. The radiographer at the Nightingale is a woman.' She injected even more enthusiasm into her voice. 'In fact, it's exciting, seeing that little shadowy shape nestling inside you, its little heart going like mad and knowing it's your baby. It's something you'll never forget.'

She remembered the tadpole-like creature that had been Thomas. She cleared her throat. 'Will your mother or partner go with you? It's fun and reassuring to have someone with whom to share the experience.'

Caroline gave a tight little laugh. 'You've got to be joking, Nurse. My partner would run a mile if I suggested that he should come—strictly a woman's province. But I might ask Ma if she'll come. Depends how busy she is.'

What was her partner, some sort of dinosaur? Strictly a woman's province? Had he never heard of being the supportive partner, sharing in the process of bonding with his child? Perhaps he didn't want this baby. Perhaps Caroline herself didn't want the baby. She was difficult to read.

Her mother had insisted that she see Oliver because he was the best. Yet she might be too busy to accompany her daughter to the hospital. They were an old county family. Was it possible that some archaic tradition about producing an heir might be in force here? Perhaps to precipitate a marriage between Caroline and her partner. It seemed ridiculous in this day and age, but one of the principles she was learning in general practice was never to be surprised.

Jessica compressed her lips. She had a nasty feeling about this pregnancy. All the signs were fine at the moment, but there was a long way to go yet. Anyway, her doubts were strong enough for her to make a note on Caroline's file and determine to discuss it with Oliver at the earliest opportunity. It looked as if Caroline was another poor little rich girl like Rachel, being left to cope on her own.

*   *   *

Mrs Avril Peters, the postnatal mum, and baby William came in for check-ups. Both passed with flying colours, but Jessica stressed that they had to come back to be examined by Oliver the following week.

'There's nothing wrong, is there?' asked Mrs Peters, looking alarmed. 'You said everything was fine.'

'Oh, it is,' assured Jessica, 'But Dr Pendragon likes to see all his postnatal cases and their babies about six weeks after birth. He just thought it might be a good idea if I saw you in the interim, iron out any small problems you might have.'

Mrs Peters beamed. 'No, there's nothing, Nurse. I can't believe I feel so fit.' She patted her abdomen, which was firming up nicely. 'Not bad for a forty-year-old primigravida, am I? I do my pelvic-floor exercises and everything else regularly. Of course, I'm lucky. My husband is marvellous. He'll do anything for William, even get up at night to change his nappy.'

'Long may it last,' said Jessica, stroking the baby's cheek. 'You're a lucky boy,' she murmured, 'to have such a loving mummy and daddy.'

William gave her a windy smile and belched.

What a daft remark to make, Jessica thought when the Peterses had left. There's nothing lucky about it. *Every* baby ought to be loved and cherished by its parents, and both father and mother should feel privileged to care for their children.

Parents and children and loving brought Oliver to mind. What was he doing right now? Had he arrived at the hospital yet? His parents lived near the Devon-Cornwall border so, depending on the traffic, it could take up to three hours to get there. He'd left their telephone number but not their address. She checked the number at the end of his note, and then did a double-take of the code... It was the same as her parents'.

So their parents lived a few miles apart at most. A tremor of disappointment trickled through her. Even last night, when he'd been unburdening himself and she had commented on the fact that their parents must live fairly near each other, he hadn't confirmed just how near. It seemed that he still didn't quite trust her. She shook her head to dismiss the unpleasant thought.

The internal phone rang. 'Lady Lyons is here,' announced Rachel.

Jessica drew in a deep breath. 'Ask her to come in, please.'

She hoped that her voice didn't give away the turmoil that was raging in her.

She liked Lady Lyons—everyone did. She was an eccentric. Oliver had a particular rapport with her.

Unescorted by Rachel, Lady Lyons limped in at great speed a moment later, entering even as she knocked.

She jerked her head toward Reception. 'Told that young woman—Rachel—not to bother. She's answering the phone. Should know the way after all these years.'

Jessica whisked round the desk in time to help her sit down. Not that she needed any help in spite of the limp.

'It's this damned ulcer,' she said, before Jessica could utter a word. Kicking the once white trainers off her bare feet, she rolled up her trouser leg and revealed a grubby, bloody bandage wrapped round her shin.

Jessica hissed in dismay. 'But that's not the dressing I put on last week.'

'No, it's the new lot of puppies—haven't got them trained yet. Wore a skirt when I went out to feed them.'

Jessica sat back on her heels. 'And they tried to make a meal of it?'

'Yep, 'fraid so.'

'When was this, Lady Lyons?'

'Day or two back.' She looked Jessica straight in the eye. 'And I rebandaged it at once.'

'So I see,' Jessica said dryly, unwrapping the amateurishly secured, many-days-old bandage to reveal an oozing, smelly mess beneath. She groaned. 'This is going to take some cleaning up, and it's not going to be very comfortable.'

Lady Lyons shrugged. 'So be it. My own fault, Nurse. You'd best get on with it.'

Jessica steered her into the treatment room, sat her in a chair with an extending footrest and sat herself on a low stool.

'I'm going to syringe out some of this purulent mess,' she explained, 'by squirting antiseptic fluid into the wound and washing out the gunge, then we'll see what else has to be done.'

'You know best, Nurse,' Lady Lyons said with a grin.

Jessica wasn't so sure when she'd cleared most of the mess, exposing the deep, slightly pink cavity. She would have liked Oliver to have been around to give an opinion. Perhaps she should have sent Lady Lyons to the Nightingale, although it was on the cards that she would have refused to go. Well, she'd started so she'd better get on with it. It was a pity that the healthy sign of a good blood inflow, which would have indicated that it was healing, wasn't present. But at least it was now reasonably clean.

She smiled up at her elderly patient's cheerful face. 'I'm going to trim away the ragged pieces of dead skin round the edges, and pack the wound with antibiotic powder, before putting on a padded protective dressing,' she said. 'And, please, Lady Lyons, if it comes adrift for whatever reason, let me know at once. Further infection and you're going to be in dead trouble.'

And so shall I, she thought, if Oliver thinks I've slipped up.

Cutting away the skin and packing the wound took some time, but at last it was finished and the stoic old lady, generous in her thanks, limped speedily out of the room.

Rachel came into the consulting room as soon as she'd seen Lady Lyons off. She was bearing two cups of coffee.

'Thanks, you're an angel,' said Jessica, though, in fact, she'd been looking forward to a few minutes alone to mull over her thoughts. 'Just give me a mo to finish this.' She scribbled a note on Lady Lyons's treatment card. 'There, that's done. I'm all yours.'

Rachel perched on the side of the desk and sipped at her coffee. 'I wonder if the boss has reached the hospital yet,' she drawled, 'and I wonder how his father is. He really looked gutted when he heard the news.'

'Unless the traffic was horrific, I think he must have reached there by now. They live in Devon. It'll probably take about three hours from here.'

Rachel raised her pencilled eyebrows. 'Devon! So that explains the accent. Though I thought it sounded rather more Cornish than Devonian.'

'Accent?'

'Mrs Pendragon, our Oliver's mother. I'd never spoken to her before. Any personal calls go through Grace if the boss isn't here, and you know how tightly her lips are buttoned where his affairs are concerned. It just seems rather odd, Mrs P. having such a strong West Country burr when he hasn't. But, then, you're from Devon and you haven't got an accent either.'

'The nuns at my convent school saw to that,' Jessica replied wryly. 'And I dare say his school did the same for Oliver.' She shifted uncomfortably. 'Look, Rachel, I don't know if we should be discussing this. It seems like an intrusion into Oliver's personal affairs, and he's such a private person. If he wanted us to know…'

Rachel went bright pink and slid off the desk. 'Oh, Lord, I don't mean to pry. I wouldn't do that. It just took me by surprise, you know, hearing her, and when she said she was Oliver's mother…' She trailed off.

'I would have been surprised, too,' said Jessica reassuringly. 'Don't worry about it. Let's just hope that we hear from Oliver soon with good news of his father.'

The words were hardly out of her mouth when the phone rang.

'Jess?' said Oliver's voice as soon as she picked up the receiver.

'Oliver,' she breathed.

Rachel mimed that she would go.

Jessica shook her head. 'No, stay,' she mouthed. She turned her attention back to Oliver. 'Have you seen your father yet?'

'Briefly. He recognised me and muttered a few slurred words. I've just left my mother with him for a bit. She's shattered but hanging in there as always. Putting on an incredibly brave face for my father. I'm waiting now to see the consultant geriatrician and find out what his assessment is.'

'Your mother must be so pleased and relieved to have you with her.'

His voice softened. 'Yes, she is.' He hesitated for a moment. 'I think you and she would get on well together, Jess. I'm looking forward to you meeting one day soon.'

Jessica was conscious of Rachel on the other side of the desk. She wished she'd let her go when she'd wanted to.

Her heart thumped painfully in her chest. Meet his mother! Had last night's revelations triggered off the idea, or had it been in his mind before then?

She said quickly, 'Rachel's here with me, wanting to know the news.'

'Good. Put her on. I must thank her for her help this morning in getting me organised.'

Jessica held out the receiver to Rachel. 'The boss wants to speak to you.'

Another pink flush washed over Rachel's beautiful face as she took the phone. 'Dr Pendragon...' Her voice was husky.

Jessica could hear Oliver speaking, but couldn't distinguish his words.

The pink flush grew deeper and a dimple appeared on either side of Rachel's perfectly lipsticked mouth. It suited her. She looked young and girlish. 'Well, thank you, Doctor, but I was only doing my duty.'

Oliver said something else which made her giggle, and then she said goodbye and handed the receiver back to Jessica. 'Sir wants a word before he goes.'

'I'll ring you tonight at home, Jess. Take care.' His voice was deep and rich and full of things left unsaid.

What was left of the afternoon flashed by. Oliver was ringing that evening. She walked on air. Whatever reservations she'd had vanished. She couldn't wait for him to phone.

CHAPTER ELEVEN

EIGHT, nine, ten o'clock passed. Jessica's heart plummeted. Oliver wasn't going to ring. He didn't want to speak to her. She had imagined his eagerness, the warmth in his voice. It had been a figment of her imagination. If he'd really cared, he would have told her that he came from Devon and not have kept her in the dark.

The telephone rang. Her hand shook as she picked up the receiver.

'Sorry I'm so late, Jess. We've only just got back from the hospital.' His voice sounded tired. She hoped he was sitting down with a large whisky in his hand.

'Your father…is he worse?'

'No, though there was a blip during the evening. His blood pressure went crazy and he became disorientated. No obvious reason. They went into action quickly enough and brought his pressure back to near normal. And they did a brain scan to eliminate a possible tumour, which might have accounted for the sudden swing in his BP. But, thank God, it was clear. Just showed what was expected, a cerebral thrombosis. He's on a nasal drip because his swallowing reflex isn't functioning properly, and he's been started on regular aspirin.'

'Oh, that's marvellous news. So it looks as if he might make a complete recovery.'

'With physio and speech therapy and lots of TLC, yes.' He paused. 'If he's got the will to make it.'

'I can't imagine your father not having the will, not if he's anything like you. Is he like you, Oliver?'

'He's twice the man I am, Jess.' He sounded fierce and rather grim.

'In that case, and with your mother's help—and she sounds a very determined lady—he'll make it. And, from what you've said, the hospital seems to be on the ball.' She paused, then said, 'I suppose it's the Old Memorial just outside of Tavistock? That must be your nearest large hospital.'

There was a small silence and then a short bark of a laugh. 'Of course. You soon sussed out from the phone code that my parents live in the same area as yours. I dare say your father uses the Memorial for his patients.'

'He does—it's our local hospital. In fact, he visits there himself when he has patients in the GP beds.' She took a deep breath which caught in her throat.

He said, 'I'm so sorry for not telling you earlier, Jess. Please forgive me. I planned to finish telling you everything tonight, clear the ground between us and make way for the future. There is a future for us together, isn't there, my love?'

His love! She kept her voice steady. 'The future. What do you mean, Oliver?'

'Our future! Why do you sound surprised?'

Her pulses raced, her palms sweated. She forced herself to play it cool. 'Because we've only known each other a few weeks, and only in the last week or so have we begun to be anything other than employer and employee. We don't know each other well enough to be talking about our future.'

'I don't think,' he said, his voice very low, 'that I ever thought of you as just an employee, though I tried damned hard to do so in those first few days. You got under my skin from the word go. As I told you—was it only yesterday? I feel as if you've always been part of me—always *will* be part of me—and you made no secret of the fact that you feel the same.'

She took in a breath from deep in her diaphragm. 'I do,' she said, unable to stop her voice from wobbling.

'Then why are you holding back?'

'I have to, until I know why you were so secretive about your parents. It's almost as if—'

'I'm ashamed of them because they're good old yeoman stock and speak with a local accent? That just isn't true, Jess. I thought I'd explained that last night. They wanted it this way for silly, outdated reasons, but they also had a stronger reason which, as promised, I'll explain when I get back.'

He sounded strained and she reminded herself that he was anxious and tired and she shouldn't add to that by pressuring him.

'I abhor the situation, but I think things may change from now on. This stroke of Dad's has put things in some sort of perspective for them and for me.' He gave a tired sigh. 'Look, love, I'll say goodnight now. Don't despair of me, Jess. I'll ring you again tomorrow. Keep both surgeries ticking over for me. Bless you.'

He rang off before she could say anything more. Furious with herself for not having been more loving, more understanding, she took herself off to bed and tossed and turned half the night.

Day followed hectic day. Jessica made herself blot out that particular conversation and made a point of being gentle and affectionate when Oliver phoned each evening.

Both surgeries were busy but it wasn't so bad in Berkley House. Rachel was able to reschedule most patients for appointments the following week in the expectation that Oliver would be back by then.

One or two people asked to see Jessica on small points relating to treatment they were already receiving or for renewal of dressings, which was routine for her. There were several patients going to out-of-the-way places for holidays or on business, already booked for injections against tropical diseases. This, too, was par for the course at Berkley House and she took it in her stride.

Oliver was missed, but the well-oiled machine could cope.

It was at Arundel Street that his presence was badly missed. As Dot said more than once, 'You don't realise how much that man does until he's not here.'

Rory lost a bit of his bounce and confidence, obviously missing Oliver's guiding hand. At the end of each surgery he drifted into Jessica's treatment room and discussed some of the trickier problems he'd had to sort during that day's surgery. Once or twice she was able to make practical suggestions that earned her his heartfelt gratitude.

'I'd not have thought of that,' he said one day, when she suggested an extra test he might order to eliminate another possible diagnosis, when trying to reach a decision on a patient presenting with a wide range of problems.

'Next time around you will,' Jessica reassured him. 'It's experience that counts in medicine and nursing. You build up a whole range of case histories that are much more accurate than any textbook. Textbooks, after all, are only guidelines—they're not infallible.'

Rory looked at her with such admiration in his eyes that she found herself blushing. 'You really are a wise lady, aren't you?' he said with a grin. 'No wonder the boss thinks that the sun rises and sets with you.'

Jessica closed the lid of the steriliser with a snap. 'He what?'

Rory's grin broadened. 'Worships you from near and from afar, adores you, lusts after you, has done since fate brought you into our midst. I'd have been in there like a shot if it hadn't been obvious. But don't mess with the boss's woman has always been my maxim.'

He was overdoing it, of course, but she felt the blood rush to and then leave her cheeks. She sat down with a bump on the stool by the bench. If Rory had noticed, then what about the others? Since day one she'd got under his skin—that's what Oliver had said, but she'd thought he'd been exaggerating. And yet it had seemingly been obvious to Rory and possibly to others.

Rory touched her arm. 'You all right, Jess? You're as white as a sheet.'

Jess! He'd called her Jess, the diminutive that she discouraged in everyone except Oliver. Joke about it, say something offbeat, anything to distract him.

'After all those kind, flattering words, Rory, what about me buying you a pie and a pint at the local, and you can flatter me some more?'

'The pie, fine, but half a shandy only. I'm on call, as I am every night at the moment.'

'What about the locum—isn't he supposed to be sharing the nights with you?'

Rory shook his head. 'Called in sick, so it's yours truly tonight and every night.'

'You can't do that. You're working hard enough during the day. Oliver won't like it.'

'Oliver won't know about it. He's got enough on his plate at the moment.'

Take care of the two surgeries, Oliver had said. She made up her mind. 'We'll get in another locum.'

Rory looked dubious. 'I don't know that I have the authority for that and good locums are few and far between.'

'Then we'll find a good one. You'll have to manage tonight, but I'll get someone in to cover tomorrow night.'

He still looked doubtful. 'But…'

Jessica smiled cheerfully. '*I've* got the authority, Rory. Now, if you're not ready for that pie and shandy, I definitely am.'

*   *   *

Jessica was determined to be rather brisk and businesslike when Oliver rang that evening. After Rory's observations about Oliver's feelings for her, she felt strangely embarrassed—on Oliver's behalf rather than her own. Did he know that he had been so transparent, and would he mind if he did know? He was usually expert at hiding his feelings.

She was anxious to get onto the business of a locum for Rory. Had she gone too far in promising that she'd find one by tomorrow night? Was this what Oliver had meant when he'd instructed her to take care of everything, or had she overstepped the mark?

He phoned at nine. He still sounded terribly tired, which was only to be expected. Visiting the sick and waiting for news, especially when one could do very little, was an exhausting business. And for Oliver, used to organising treatment rather than having to leave it to someone else, it had to be particularly frustrating.

As always, she opened by asking after his father. He gave her an update.

'He's responding to physio and speech therapy,' he told her, 'though there's some anxiety about a possible deep vein thrombosis in his left leg. They've started him on a low dose of heparin which, with the aspirin, ought to produce results quite soon. Of course, it's a balancing trick—too much heparin and you might have a bleed, too little and you lose control of the thrombosis. Tomorrow he's to have more chest X-rays and another ECG.' He added, sounding quite cheerful, 'Believe me, it's all go.'

Jess chuckled softly. 'My father says that being a patient in hospital is an exhausting business—you have to work so hard.'

'He's dead right. Now, love, what's the news from your end? All well?'

It was amazing how he managed to sound tender and loving even when tired and talking facts and medicine. Would he still sound the same after she'd come clean about her promise to Rory? Taking a deep breath, she plunged straight into the business of a night locum.

Concisely, she explained the situation and waited, holding her breath, with butterflies fluttering in her stomach and chest.

She let out her breath in a great whoosh when he said calmly, 'Good. I'm glad you were firm with Rory. You're absolutely right—we must get in another locum. I'd rather avoid the agency. You could try Dr Ian MacDonald—he's semi-retired, but a game old thing. Ask Grace Talbot to look him up in my personal diary, but I want *you* to speak to him and explain things, then get Rory to bring him up to date about the patients.'

'Won't Mrs Talbot be offended if I talk to the doctor? After all, she is your personal secretary.'

'Not at all. She thinks very highly of you and will consider this a medical matter that you should deal with. Now, go to bed and sleep well. Goodnight, my love, and thanks for holding the fort so competently.'

All the gentleness and tenderness in his voice made tears prick the back of her eyes. She suddenly felt incredibly lonely, and longed to feel his arms round her, hugging her to him as he had when she'd told him about Thomas. 'Any idea when you'll be back?' she asked, wondering if he could hear the tears in her voice, sense how bereft she felt.

'I'll be home by Sunday, if all continues to go well. Are you missing me, Jess?'

'Yes,' she breathed. 'I'm missing you very much.'

She would have liked to have asked if he missed her, but couldn't get the words out. Not that it mattered, she realised with a surge of supreme happiness. He didn't need to say it.

Jessica missed Oliver more over the next few days and nights. The sight of his dark head bent over a patient when he was doing an examination. The sound of his voice, deep and vibrant and reassuring. The masculine smell of him which she could never quite pin down. She longed with a dull ache low down in her loins for him to come back and make love to her.

It was a longing she hadn't experienced since she was two months pregnant with Thomas, and his father had walked out on her. At first she had missed him, but it had been nothing like this.

It hadn't *hurt*, the way this longing for Oliver hurt. It had been nothing. She hadn't felt as if part of herself had been missing. And yet she and Oliver hadn't even made love— they hadn't had the time or opportunity for sex. For right or wrong reasons they'd held back, fought the vibes that had been pulling them together. Now there was no need to fight.

* * *

She couldn't sleep on Saturday night, and Sunday seemed to take for ever to arrive, yet when it did it took her by surprise. There was so much to do. Oh, come off it, she chided herself. What is there to do, except to prepare a meal? The cottage was spotless. She'd vacuumed and dusted and polished yesterday and everything gleamed.

She hadn't a clue whether he was arriving—morning, afternoon or evening—but whenever he came he would be hungry. She decided on a ham salad and warm French bread, which would do for lunch or supper. By nine o'clock she had tossed a large bowl of chopped lettuce, watercress, cucumber, green peppers and salad onions, decorating it with flower-shaped cherry tomatoes and radishes and rings of red onions—a fiddly finishing touch of colour. The cut-glass bowl went into the fridge to chill and crisp up.

She mixed the special vinaigrette, which her mother had taught her to make, to add later.

There was also a bottle of dry white wine chilling in the fridge. It was standing alongside the champagne he'd brought on his previous visit and which they'd not opened.

Preparing the salad and laying the table was a time-consuming labour of love—well, why not? But whoever thought that salad was an easy meal to prepare had never put together a salad prepared the Mrs Friday way. It would look fantastic at the centre of the polished table. A real eye-catcher. Better than flowers.

She was still bubbling over with adrenaline and anticipation when everything was as ready as it could be. For starters they would have mushroom soup out of a carton—gingered up with a few herbs, it really did taste home-made. For pudding, the fudge cake, a speciality of the local baker, loaded with calories but delicious.

What if Oliver came for lunch and stayed for supper? She would have to rustle up two meals. But it wasn't the thought of producing two meals that made her heart turn over and over in her chest and her stomach clench. If he stayed for supper…

She felt breathless in spite of the cool October morning. She would go for a walk along the shore, breathe in some fresh, salty air, kick a few pebbles—that always calmed her.

She kicked a few pebbles, then took off her sandals and rolled up her jeans and splashed along in the shallow water, icy cold in spite of the pale sunshine. Slowly she ambled toward the end of the spit. It was low tide and, except for the occasional screaming of gulls as they circled overhead and the lapping of tiny waves rippling up the sand, very quiet.

It was like being at the end of the world, she thought, sitting down on the drying sand above the low-water mark. Along the coast, a mile or so away, the domed silver pier at Porthampton glittered in the morning sunlight. Way out to sea, a couple of large liners were silhouetted on the horizon, waiting for the tide to change so that they could sail into the docks beyond the pier.

Jessica looked at her watch. It was still only ten o'clock. What on earth could she do to kill time until he arrived? The garden. She would do something in the garden—that would keep her busy, stop her wondering how they would greet each other, give her a chance to appear calm and relaxed when he arrived. Of course, if that wasn't until the afternoon...

'Hello, Jess, you look like that mermaid in Copenhagen harbour, lost in thought, gazing out to sea.'

At the sound of his voice she froze. Then slowly she turned her head. Oliver stood in the shallow water a few yards away, his cords rolled up to his muscular calves with their scattering of dark hairs, his white shirt unbuttoned to the waist. The sun gleamed on his lightly tanned face and black hair. A patch over one eye, she thought, and he'd double for a pirate in a forties movie.

Would her heart ever return to where it should be? She let her breath out on a long sigh. Be cool, be calm. 'You've forgotten your cutlass,' she said dryly. 'And a colourful cummerbund wouldn't come amiss.'

Grey eyes glinted, his eyebrows shot up, his mouth quirked at the corners. 'Enlighten me— you've lost me.'

Jess smiled, trying for an enigmatic, Mona Lisa-type smile. 'My joke, it doesn't matter.' She found that she could stand up. She dusted the sand off her bottom, hoping that he wouldn't notice that her legs were shaking.

His eyes swept over her. He took a few steps forward and opened his arms wide. 'Come here, Jess.' It was a command, though his voice was barely above a whisper.

For an instant she hesitated.

'Come,' he repeated.

She splashed toward him and felt his arms close round her.

His body was rock hard against hers. Her softness was moulded to his hardness. Her hands crept up his bare chest, fanned out over his smooth shoulders, slid up into his thick, crisp hair. She lifted her face, he bent his head. 'I love you, Jess,' he murmured, as his mouth closed over hers.

They stood there for a long time, murmuring, hands stroking, exploring, body to body, heart to heart, mouth to mouth—unaware of the screaming, wheeling gulls or the changing tide.

Jess noticed it first. She eased herself away from him. 'My jeans,' she said in a surprised voice, 'are getting wet. The tide's coming in.'

Oliver swept her up in his arms. 'We can't have that,' he said. His voice was husky, his eyes smouldering. 'We'd better get you back to the cottage and out of those wet pants.'

Jess giggled, a frivolous, girlish giggle. 'Are you being suggestive, propositioning me?'

'You'd better believe it,' said Oliver, striding through the water.

'You can put me down now. I can walk along the dry sand.'

Oliver didn't even bother to answer.

They reached the cottage.

'Where's your key?' he asked.

He wasn't even breathless, Jess noticed.

'It's on the latch—we don't get thieves and vandals on the Spit. It's safe to leave doors unlocked.'

He elbowed open the door and edged through it, then kicked it behind him and carried her straight up the narrow staircase.

A ribbon of pale sunshine slanted across the bed.

Carefully Oliver placed her in the ribbon of light. Jess lay perfectly still, her eyes locked with his. He knelt over her, his knees grazing her hips, his back straight, his head bent to look down at her. Now he *was* breathing heavily and his grey eyes were as dark as granite. Large and commanding, predatory, he loomed over her.

Jess waited for him to shower her with passionate kisses, undress her, toss her clothes aside, make love to her. It had been so long.

She quivered with her need of him, her breath coming in quick, shallow inhalations. He didn't move.

She moistened her lips with the tip of her tongue. 'Oliver?'

He half smiled. 'So what is it to be, Jess, confession time or loving time?' His voice was gruff.

Was he teasing? Was this part of his kind of foreplay?

'You don't know what I'm talking about, do you, my love?'

The 'my love' was reassuring. She couldn't speak. She shook her head, her eyes pleading.

He dropped a swift kiss on her forehead. 'No loving, you said, until I came clean about my murky past—all of it. So does that rule still apply? Your choice, Jess.'

Could he really stop now? His arousal was obvious, had been since they'd been entwined together on the beach. Hers must be obvious, too—the sheen of sweat on her face and neck, the way she had thrust against him, the way now she was unable to stop arching up to him, the way her nipples peaked. Her body had a life of its own.

She moistened her lips again. 'No choice,' she murmured. 'I love you whatever—please, love me now.'

Oliver's love-making swooped and soared, between gentle tracing with lips and sensitive fingers the swells and crevasses of her body, making her sigh and tremble and gasp with pleasure, to penetrating, thrusting movements deep within her that had her pleading for fulfilment.

And Jess found herself responding with a wildness that she hadn't known she possessed. Her own lips and hands and teeth were busy, rousing Oliver to greater heights. He gave little grunts of pain and pleasure, giving her nip for nip with his own strong teeth.

Their hungry love-making came together in a stream of rhythmic mutual peaks of pure delight. Satiated at last, they fell asleep, with Jess cupped into the curve of his body as he wrapped himself round behind her.

The wall clock in the tiny hall chimed four as they sat down to the ham salad and warm French bread. They'd made love in bed, and again in the shower when they'd woken at two.

Each time there had been subtleties which had made their love-making different and fresh.

They were halfway through the salad when Jess said, 'I forgot the mushroom soup.'

'It doesn't matter,' said Oliver. He dipped a forkful of ham into herb mustard. 'I'm starving, I couldn't have waited for soup to be heated. Let's have it for supper, I'll be more than ready for it then. This love-making is hungry business, I'll need to get stoked up again.' His eyes had that special glint in them that made her melt.

'Oh,' she murmured, unaccountably going pink, 'are you staying for supper and...?'

'Especially the ''and'' if I'm invited.'

She went a deeper shade of pink, but didn't answer directly. 'For the first time in a long, long time,' she said softly, 'I feel complete, but...'

Oliver moved round the table and folded her in his arms. He knew exactly what she needed to hear. 'We'll never forget Thomas,' he whispered. 'However many other children we have, he'll always be part of that completeness.'

She went very still in his arms. He brushed a kiss across her forehead. 'That is by way of being a proposal,' he said. 'Will you marry me, Jess?'

Her heart hammered against her ribs. This was what she had longed to hear, but did she dare so soon? They still knew so little about each other. Though Oliver now knew more of her than she did of him. There was still that blank, that secret in his life. It shouldn't have niggled, but it did. Yet their love-making had been perfect, a revelation. Surely it wouldn't have been like that if they weren't meant for each other. It hadn't been just sex, but something much, much deeper than that.

She'd made one mistake, chosen the wrong man. Thomas had turned that fiasco into heaven for a few months. But could she risk it again? A wedding ring wasn't a cast-iron guarantee of love and fidelity.

Oliver nuzzled the top of her head. 'Shall we go and sit comfortably?' he said. 'And I'll fill in that gap.' He released her, took her hand and led her to the squashy sofa.

How *did* he always know what to say and do?

'I don't have to know,' she assured him, sinking down onto the sofa. 'I love you,

Oliver, with all my heart. It's because I love you that I have doubts. I couldn't bear—'

'Neither could I. We have something precious, we must hang onto it. No secrets, no prevaricating. My life is your life, Jess.'

He poured the last of the wine and sat down beside her. He started abruptly as she had when telling her story.

'I haven't told you about Simon, have I?'

A strange expression flitted across his face which she couldn't fathom, a mixture of sadness and anger she thought.

'Simon?'

'My brother, two years younger than I.' He drained his glass, stood up and walked over to the window overlooking the back garden. 'Simon had learning difficulties, and was— could be at times—aggressive, due to frustration, I guess. When we were both small he followed me around and I could manage him better than anyone, but as we got older...' His voice trailed off. 'You haven't by any chance got anything stronger, have you?' He motioned to his empty glass. His distress was clear.

Jess got up. 'I have. Dad's a great believer in a spot of medicinal whisky when the going's hard.'

She disappeared into the kitchen for a moment and was back in a flash. 'Here.' She handed him a half-full tumbler. 'You don't have to go on.' She pressed his arm and reached up and kissed him.

He squeezed her hand. 'I want to, Jess. I should have told you earlier, before I asked you to marry me. It's a relief to unload after all these years of keeping quiet.'

Jess returned to the sofa. That's how she'd felt when telling him about Thomas. 'Go on,' she said softly, 'and, for the record, nothing you have to say will make any difference to me wanting to marry you.'

He produced a rather grim little smile. 'You'd better hear the rest. As we got older, Simon became jealous of me and his hero-worship turned to hatred. Understandable. Poor chap, he must have felt second best in everything. He had the clothes that I'd grown out of, was backward at school and I was pretty bright. Mum and Dad were marvellous, but were working all hours…'

He sipped his whisky. 'I tried to help him with his reading, but he didn't want to know. One day he lashed out at me with a pen-knife…'

'So that's where that scar on your arm came from. I often wondered.'

Oliver looked surprised. 'Fancy you noticing that.'

Jessica said softly, 'Don't you understand? I notice everything about you, Oliver. It's a pretty deep scar. It must have needed stitches. How did you explain it to the hospital staff?'

'Told them we'd been mucking about and it had happened accidentally. They swallowed it, but Mum and Dad didn't. That's why, when I won the scholarship, they somehow found the money towards my board. Ironically, if it hadn't happened and I hadn't had to go to Casualty, I probably wouldn't be here. I watched the casualty officer stitching up my arm, and knew that I wanted to be a doctor.

'And Simon's condition attracted me to medicine, too. Over the years he got worse— graduating from shoplifting to mugging and GBH, and from short sentences to longer ones. And increasingly pieces appeared in the local paper about him. When I was starting to build up my private practice my parents begged me stop visiting. Pendragon is a fairly distinguished name on the borders, and they were afraid that if the press got hold of the fact that

I was a consultant—well, you can guess the rest.'

He swallowed more whisky. 'Of course, I wouldn't stop seeing them, but I agreed to keep a low profile. It was nonsense, but I had to go along with it—they had made so many sacrifices for me. All they wanted was for me to be a success and, I guess, make up for Simon. But I hated it, Jess. I felt a traitor and a coward, being unable to acknowledge my parents. Yet it was what they wanted.'

He walked restlessly about the room, before turning to face her. 'Simon moved to London, and disappeared. I tried to trace him with private detectives, but had no luck. Then, five years ago, the police contacted my parents. He had been arrested for killing someone in a fight over drugs.' His voice was colourless but his eyes were deep, grey pools of distress.

Jess felt as if she'd been kicked in the stomach. She felt the blood drain from her face. 'He killed someone…'

'Yes,' said Oliver. 'In a fit of rage, my brother killed another human being…' He held out his hands, palms upwards. 'And, as a doctor, *I* should have prevented it, Jess.' His face was ravaged, drawn. 'I should have done more to help Simon.'

CHAPTER TWELVE

OLIVER stood with his back to the window, silhouetted against the fading afternoon sunlight. Jessica couldn't see his face, but could hear the pain and anguish in his voice.

She shivered. It was getting chilly. She rose like a zombie and moved to the fireplace. She put a match to the waiting logs and stayed crouching down to make sure that they had caught.

'I pride myself on laying a fire the way my father used to lay our camping fires—no fire-lighters, just twisted paper and shavings.' The meaningless words spilled out.

Oliver moved away from the window and came and crouched down beside her.

'You're in shock,' he said. 'Have some of this.' He tilted the glass of whisky against her lips.

Jessica allowed a little to trickle down her throat. The logs began to crackle as tiny flames licked round them. Oliver put an arm round her waist and pulled her to her feet.

She leaned against him. 'Your poor parents. Two sons so different—one saving life, one taking it.'

Oliver's arm tightened round her waist. 'I've often wondered whether if I'd been honest about Simon knifing me, he might have been given some help.'

Jessica gathered her wits together. For the first time she spoke deliberately. 'You know that now, with professional hindsight, but as a child you thought you were protecting him. And your parents thought that they could deal with it, or they would have involved the authorities. For heaven's sake, my darling, don't feel guilty about it.' She emphasised the words. It was important that he didn't add more guilt to the load he already carried.

Tenderly she ran a finger round his lips as if to seal them.

Oliver steered her back to the sofa and said hesitantly, 'Does the ''my darling'' mean that marriage is still on the cards, in spite of...?'

Jessica sat bolt upright. 'It was never in doubt,' she snapped. 'I told you that, whatever you had to say, it would make no difference.'

'But you didn't expect to find yourself tied up with someone whose brother was a killer—did you?'

She took several deep breaths. He suddenly sounded hard, cynical, almost as if he was offering a way out, wanting her to back off. She had to find the right words to break through to him.

'No, but neither did you expect to find a woman who'd been traumatised into a breakdown by the death of her baby. Yet your love was strong enough to take that on board. What makes you think that my love for you can't cope with a sick brother who needs help rather than condemnation?' Her voice was remarkably cool and even.

'Needed, not needs—Simon's dead. He committed suicide whilst on remand, awaiting trial, though the charge had been reduced to manslaughter. We had a good lawyer who might even have got him off, or had him admitted into psychiatric care. But his guilt wouldn't let him live. I saw him the day before he took his own life. He was like the small, good-natured child who had followed me around. Sorry for what he'd done, wanting to make up for it.'

His eyes were like bleak, grey pools. 'Sounds impossible, doesn't it, this complete about-face? Like Saul on the road to Damascus. But that's the way it is with people with my brother's mental imbalance. It was a bitter-sweet visit. I wasn't happy about him and asked the prison doctor if he could be moved to the sick bay, even if it was just for the night. But he dismissed the idea that there was anything wrong. He seemed to know his stuff. He was the expert. I let him convince me, but I've always despised myself for not insisting on the move.'

Jessica thought that her heart would stop. There seemed to be no end to Simon's harrowing story. 'Surely they kept a special eye on him after you'd expressed your concern.'

'Apparently not. He was discovered by the warder who opened his cell door the following morning—he'd been dead a long time.'

'How—how did he die?'

'Hung himself.'

Tears spilled down Jessica's cheeks. 'Oh, Oliver, how awful for you and your parents after everything else. And poor Simon, all on his own...'

Oliver gathered her into his arms and wiped her eyes with a large handkerchief. He was comforting her again. 'You know,' he said, 'once my parents got over the initial agony of Simon's suicide they were strangely relieved. To them, he was at peace at last. That I had seen him the day before was a huge comfort to them. I was able to tell them that he loved them, was full of remorse for what he'd done, for how he'd behaved all his adult life.'

'But how do you feel, Oliver?'

'How...do...I...feel?' He dragged the words out.

It was as if no one had ever asked him about his feelings—they probably hadn't. Jessica guessed that to his parents he was almost as much a mystery as their younger son. He was brilliant and had long ago moved out of their sphere of influence. He moved in circles that they couldn't, wouldn't want to aspire to. It probably hadn't crossed their minds that he might sometimes be unsure of himself, need to be comforted.

'Yes, as in how do you feel about your brother's death, apart from feeling guilty? Are you relieved it's all over? Do you think Simon's at peace?'

He took hold of her hand and kissed her knuckles. 'I'm relieved,' he said slowly. 'Glad that his unhappy life is over. But I haven't my parents' deep religious faith. I go to church occasionally, believe in the power of prayer, though in the face of what we see in medicine I find it sometimes hard.'

Jessica planted a kiss in the centre of his palm and then folded his fingers over it. She said softly, 'That's exactly how I feel. But I firmly believe one of the bits in the New Testament.'

'What bit's that?'

'Where Jesus said, ''Suffer the little children to come to me.'' I think that would apply to Simon and people like him who have never really grown up.'

'Oh, my dear Jess.' He drew her into his arms and brushed kisses on her upturned face. 'Thank you, love, thank you for that. Only you could have thought of something so comforting. You know, I wanted to take the prison doctor to court—in fact, I wanted to take them all to court, the whole prison service—but my parents begged me not to. They were right. It would have taken years, and to what purpose? As Dad said, let Simon rest in peace. Much better to do something constructive in his memory.'

She had one of her flashes of inspiration. 'And that's when you opened the Arundel Street surgery, as a sort of memorial to Simon and a thank you to your parents.'

He smiled slightly. 'How did you guess?'

She wanted to say, Because I love you and understand your generous spirit. Instead, she said, 'The timing was right. You started the surgery about five years ago.' She stroked his cheek, and with her forefinger traced the tiny network of tired lines around his eyes.

'It explains so much that has puzzled me since I joined the practice. Like why you are so protective of your Arundel Street patients. Patients like little Naomi and the rest of the Walker family, gorgeous Gloria and the grandparents. And what about all those people you write letters for to rotten landlords and councils? That's way beyond the call of duty.'

Oliver opened his mouth to say something, but Jessica placed her hand over it.

'No, let me say what I want to say, love. Accept a bit of praise gracefully from your future wife.'

'I like that,' he murmured against her palm. 'Future wife.'

Jessica wasn't to be sidetracked. 'It explains why you are reluctant to notify the police about the awful Barry Woods selling pot to his classmates. He reminds you of Simon, except that, unlike Simon, he is too clever by half and comes from a deprived background. As you said the other day, what chance has the boy had with a gaolbird for a father and a battered mother to protect?'

'I have nightmares about Barry sometimes,' Oliver admitted. 'I'm not into breaking the law, but I want to do what's best for the boy and his mother. After what happened to Simon in prison, I'm not sure what to do about him. Ideally I should like to—'

His mobile buzzed. His face lit up. 'That'll be my mother with news of Dad.'

'I'll go through to the kitchen,' Jess mouthed as he answered the call.

He shook his head and grabbed her hand as she went to stand up. He covered the mouthpiece. 'Don't go. I want you to speak to Mum after she's filled me in about Dad. Hello, Mum,' he said when Jess sank back down beside him. 'Tell me all about Dad.'

There were the usual muffled tones of someone at the other end of the phone, and then Oliver said, 'So there's already some improvement in the thrombosis in his leg, and he was able to walk a few steps with a frame. Oh, that's great news—'

The voice at the other end interrupted. 'No, Mum, it won't hurt him at all to be walking— he's not being pushed too fast. It's the latest treatment for strokes, to get patients on their feet as soon as possible.'

Again something was said at the other end. Oliver laughed. 'Mum, you're a glutton for punishment. Dad isn't ready to go home yet— it's less than a week since he had the stroke— but I'll ring Keith Redman tomorrow and see if he can give me any idea when he might be able to go home.'

He listened to something else that his mother was saying. Then he said, 'Yes, I'm at her cottage and, yes, she's said yes.' With a broad smile, he handed the mobile to Jessica. 'My mum wants to speak to you,' he said.

Jess went from pink to red and back to white. 'Your mother knows about us,' she breathed.

'She does, and she's thrilled. We spent several night vigils by Dad's bedside. Very conducive to confession. We came closer than we've ever been.' He pushed the instrument into her hand. 'Speak to her, Jess, please.'

They talked for ten minutes, easily, frankly, as if they were old friends. It was rather like talking to her own mother, Jess thought. It ended with her promising that she would visit as soon as possible.

'I suppose,' she said, handing Oliver back his mobile, 'that I'd better put my parents in the picture, but I don't know how on earth—'

Her phone rang.

She jumped. 'That'll be them.' She was breathless. 'They often ring about this time on a Sunday… Oh, Oliver, what shall I say?'

Oliver nibbled her ear. 'I'll tell you what to say if you get stuck.'

He handed her the receiver. Her mother's disembodied voice floated into the room. Jessica held the receiver a few inches from her ear so that Oliver could listen in. 'Hello, darling, you were a long time answering. Were you in the garden?'

'No, Mum. Is Dad with you?'

'As always, he's waiting to speak to you. Why, have you something special to say to both of us?'

'Oh, Mum, how do you always know?'

'Because she's a witch,' her father's voice came from an extension. 'A white witch, I'm pleased to say. Give her long enough and she'll be able to suss out what you have to tell us without any help from you.'

Oliver's eyebrows shot up. His eyes twinkled. Soundlessly he mouthed, 'Ask your mother if she *can* guess.'

Before Jessica could speak her mother said, 'You've someone with you.'

'How do you know that?'

'I can sense him.' She chuckled. 'And you've taken your time replying.'

Jessica took a deep breath. 'How do you know it's a him, Mum?'

Her father answered. 'Because you've something special to tell us. Because whenever you've phoned you've been holding something back. Because you didn't need our help when you moved into the cottage. Because you are so obviously happy and have at last laid your past to rest. Even I, a mere man, without your mother's witchery, have been able to deduce that much. Need I say more?'

Oliver prised the receiver from Jessica's white fingers. 'Dr Friday, sir, this is Oliver Pendragon. Jessica has done me the honour of agreeing to be my wife. We haven't known each other for long, but—'

'Time isn't important,' cut in Mrs Friday. 'Gerry and I knew within days.'

Jessica snatched the receiver from Oliver. 'Mum, we want to come down as soon as possible. I can't wait for you to meet Oliver. And we're going to meet his parents, too—they only live a few miles away. Mr Pendragon is in the Memorial at the moment, recovering from a stroke.'

'I've got to go in and see a couple of patients there tomorrow,' said her father. 'I'll introduce myself, if that's OK with Oliver.'

'I'd be grateful, Dr Friday,' said Oliver.

'The name's Gerry,' replied the doctor.

As soon as the phone was put down, Oliver took Jessica into his arms. 'Your eyes are shining like stars,' he murmured. He dropped random kisses on her face and neck.

Jessica kissed him back. 'So are yours,' she whispered.

They sank down onto the sofa, then rolled down onto the rug in front of the fire.

'Don't you think it's rather warm?' said Oliver in a chuckly voice. He pulled off his sweater. His chest, and the cluster of dark hairs arrowing down to disappear into the waistband of his trousers, glistened in the firelight.

Jessica pulled her T-shirt over her head. Oliver kissed her armpits and she collapsed in a heap. 'My most ticklish spot.' She giggled.

'I'll remember that,' he said softly, nuzzling her bare breasts and unbuttoning her jeans.

The logs had died down to a red glow when they woke an hour or so later. The windows were dark, the sky full of stars.

Oliver snaked out an arm and threw some fresh logs on the red embers.

'I've never made love on a rug in front of a fire before,' she whispered, as he pulled her to him again.

'I should hope not,' he said indignantly. 'It's not the sort of behaviour I would expect my future wife to have indulged in.'

'Talking of being your future wife, how and when are we going to break the news to the two surgeries?'

'How.' Oliver reached for his discarded cords and pulled a small box from a pocket. Inside, on a ruby velvet bed, lay an antique ring of such beauty that Jess could only stare at it speechlessly. 'With this, my love.' He slipped the ring on her finger, where a cluster of blue sapphires glowed in an intricate silver oval setting. 'Wear it to work tomorrow and it will break the news for us.'

At Berkley House, Rachel, Mrs Lemon and even Grace Talbot drooled over it.

'A beautiful ring,' praised Grace. 'Very distinctive, more restrained than diamonds. But that's what one would expect of the doctor—he's a man of great taste.'

'It's beautiful,' breathed Rachel, and Mrs Lemon agreed.

Jessica knew that they were right.

It was the same at Arundel Street that afternoon. Jane and Dorothy, and a couple of patients who were waiting to be seen, oohed and aahed over its beauty. Rory came through from his consulting room to call for his next patient, and was impressed.

'Just the sort of thing the boss would get for his lady,' he said, and winked at Jessica.

Even Fred Stone had noticed it when she'd arrived to park in the yard. 'About time the boss got hitched, and quite right it's to you, miss. You're well suited.'

How did he know that? wondered Jessica.

Every female patient Jessica saw that afternoon wanted to see the ring. She kept hauling it out from beneath her uniform dress where it hung on the silver chain which Oliver had had the forethought to give her.

'I wouldn't keep it hidden like that,' said Gwen Stowe, who had come in to have her suppurating varicose ulcer re-dressed. 'I'd be flashing it around, beautiful ring like that. Must have cost a bomb.'

'But not very practical to wear when I'm working,' said Jessica with a smile as she gently peeled away the messy dressing.

'Let's get married soon,' said Oliver that evening as they sat in front of the fire, leaning against the sofa. 'Before Christmas. I don't see any point in hanging about. We love each other. There's nothing more to say.'

'Mmm,' Jess murmured, closing her eyes and letting the flickering flames warm her face. 'I'd like to be married in our village church—

unless you'd rather it was here in a registry office. It might be more convenient for Rachel and the others, and I'd like them all to come.'

Oliver kissed her eyes open. 'Wouldn't dream of tying the knot without them. Let's make it a Saturday—easier to arrange half-day cover. I'm sure they'd all enjoy a trip to Devon, even in midwinter.' He gave her the special smile that was for her alone, and she melted into his arms.

EPILOGUE

IT WAS mid-afternoon when Jess and Oliver drove out of the little Devon village. They gave a final wave to the crowd on the hotel steps. The December sun was low in the sky, a pale disc almost on the horizon. It had remained cold all day, and frost still glittered on the roof of the squat little village church where a few hours before they had been married.

Jess sighed. 'It was a lovely wedding, with all our friends and relatives there,' she said softly. 'But I'm glad it's over and I've got you to myself for a whole fortnight.'

'You looked out of this world,' Oliver murmured. 'Stunning in your wedding dress. It was soft and golden and looked like clotted cream. You looked good enough to eat.' He smacked his lips. 'Mmm.'

Jess chuckled. 'Well, you know the old adage—the way to a man's heart...'

'I expect you to be a well-informed, modern wife who knows all about cholesterol, and will look after my arteries and not overfeed me.'

The slip road to the motorway was quiet. He planted a quick kiss on her cheek.

' "Be careful, it's my heart," ' she crooned.

'Don't know that one. Sounds like an oldie.' He edged into the traffic on the motorway.

'It is. Gran sings it a lot. Apparently it was a favourite in the forties, all dreamy and nostalgic like a lot of songs were then. She's got loads of old records of that period. The fact that we're going to New Orleans for our honeymoon pleased her no end. You've got good taste, she reckons, to take me to the home of soul and jazz.'

'She's a lovely lady. It was a privilege to meet her. Do you realise...' he gave her his special sideways grin '...that one day we'll have grandchildren of our own, and they might be talking about us like this?'

They were cruising steadily in the middle lane.

'Hey, aren't you forgetting something—like it's children before grandchildren?' said Jess.

His grin widened. 'No, my darling, I'm not forgetting all that begetting and begetting—the fun bit, especially after these weeks of abstinence.' He was suddenly serious and took his hand from the steering-wheel for an instant to cover hers. 'I'm so glad, Jess, that you want to start a family straight away. This is one boss who'll be delighted to grant maternity leave to his much valued super nurse—and the sooner the better.'

Jess closed her eyes and smiled her Mona Lisa smile. She folded her hands across her abdomen. 'I can't wait,' she whispered, 'to have your baby. I know it's fashionable for a woman to work for a couple of years, establish her career or climb the ladder, but I don't want to do that. At least for a year or two I want to be a full-time mother.'

Oliver half turned to give her a smile. He said softly, 'Remind me from time to time to tell you what a wonderful woman you are. I wasn't sure how you felt about having another baby in the near future. I thought that you might want to wait. We'll start it on our honeymoon—it'll be a real love baby.'

'They'll all be true love babies,' she said.

Oliver heaved a deep satisfied sigh. 'I can just see them, a whole tribe of silver-haired kids like their mum.'

'They'll have black hair like their dad.'

'I shall insist on silver.'

Jess smiled gently. 'Darling, I know that you're the world's greatest obstetrician, but I don't think even you can arrange that one.'

Oliver gave a shout of laughter. 'You're dead right, love. DNA will out and, anyway, who cares if they're ginger pink as long as they are healthy and whole?'

'As you say, who cares?' said Jess. She leaned across and kissed his cheek. 'Thank you for making me so happy.'

'Making you happy, dear heart,' said Oliver softly, 'will be my pleasure and privilege—always.'

MEDICAL ROMANCE™

Large Print

Titles for the next three months...

March

JUMPING TO CONCLUSIONS	Judy Campbell
FINGER ON THE PULSE	Abigail Gordon
THE MOST PRECIOUS GIFT	Anne Herries
THE TIME IS NOW	Gill Sanderson

April

JUST A FAMILY DOCTOR	Caroline Anderson
ONE AND ONLY	Josie Metcalfe
LIFTING SUSPICION	Gill Sanderson
PARTNERS FOR LIFE	Lucy Clark

May

PARTNERS FOR EVER	Lucy Clark
TWO'S COMPANY	Josie Metcalfe
THE BEST MAN	Helen Shelton
ON THE RIGHT TRACK	Rebecca Lang

MILLS & BOON®

Makes any time special™